The Boy from Left Field

THE BOY FROM LEFT FIELD

Tom Henighan

DUNDURN
TORONTO

Editor: Allison Hirst
Design: Courtney Horner
Printer: Webcom

Library and Archives Canada Cataloguing in Publication

Henighan, Tom
The boy from left field / Tom Henighan.

Issued also in electronic formats.
ISBN 978-1-4597-0060-4

I. Title.

PS8565.E582B69 2012 jC813'.54 C2011-903853-6

1 2 3 4 5 16 15 14 13 12

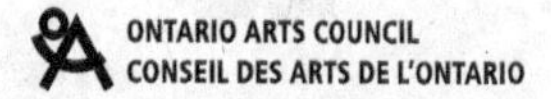

We acknowledge the support of the **Canada Council for the Arts** and the **Ontario Arts Council** for our publishing program. We also acknowledge the financial support of the **Government of Canada** through the **Canada Book Fund** and **Livres Canada Books**, and the **Government of Ontario** through the **Ontario Book Publishing Tax Credit** and the **Ontario Media Development Corporation**.

Care has been taken to trace the ownership of copyright material used in this book. The author and the publisher welcome any information enabling them to rectify any references or credits in subsequent editions.

J. Kirk Howard, President

Printed and bound in Canada.
www.dundurn.com

Dundurn
3 Church Street, Suite 500
Toronto, Ontario, Canada
M5E 1M2

Gazelle Book Services Limited
White Cross Mills
High Town, Lancaster, England
LA1 4XS

Dundurn
2250 Military Road
Tonawanda, NY
U.S.A. 14150

For Cathy and Marilyn, and all the kids they inspired — and who inspired them — in the unforgettable "Room 27"

The children run so fast.
They want to beat the throw
of time and trouble.
They want to touch home plate,
even sliding.

And sometimes fate lies low
and time's in hiding —
then the winning run is sweet,
as children know,
even sliding.

Chapter 1

Home in a Taxi

Once upon a time, not very long ago, a boy named Hawk lived with his mother in a taxicab on a grey and grim street in Toronto, just east of the Don River.

If you don't know Toronto, let me tell you that the Don flows through the eastern part of the city and into Lake Ontario. It rolls through a valley once used up and worn out by generations of people too busy working for a living to bother with clean water, noble trees, or rolling green fields.

The valley is greener now and the river, once horribly polluted, is beginning to look like a river again. Just east of its still-murky waters, however, some poor neighbourhoods hang on and shelter people who can't afford the fine houses that lie north, around the fine old avenue called the Danforth.

The taxicab Hawk and his mother called home

didn't zip around the city picking up passengers. It was a huge 1980s Oldsmobile station wagon, and it had seen better days. Once loaded with features, the car was a wreck. Its body was half rusted out, the engine had been stripped of everything valuable, the fake leather seats were full of holes, and you could see the patchy ground through the rotted metal floor.

This relic sat in a big, dusty yard surrounded by crumbling brick warehouses and next to some hunks of rusting machinery. A couple of Dumpsters parked beside the road enclosed the space and made it almost private.

A few feet from the car was the back of an old brick building, still in use. If you walked through the door and into the dark hallway you could smell curry, sweet spices, scents of tea and baked nan. There was an Indian restaurant facing out on the next street, and it was very much alive and popular, not only with the neighbourhood people, but with residents for miles around. The owner, whose name was Selim, took pity on Hawk and his mother, and let them live in his back lot and use the washrooms and some of the facilities of the restaurant. He sent out an occasional bowl of rice, some leftover pakoras, or even a delicious sweet, like Gulab Jamun, when he thought they might be short of food.

Hawk was ten years old and should have been in school, but his mother was having a fight with his teacher, and refused to let him go anywhere near his grade four class. Hawk's mother, who had decided on her own account that she was a Native person, called herself Storm Cloud, which was an appropriate name for a woman who raised a fuss about everything and caused trouble in order to get what she wanted, even when she didn't have to.

One rainy morning in May, when Hawk was getting bored with his street life and the cramped taxi, he decided that he wanted to go back to school.

He ran around the old car, jumping over puddles and waving his arms and shouting, "Look, Ma, it's a terrible day. I can't play stickball with Mr. Rizzuto, and there's no point in going to the park. At school I could at least read a book."

His mother, who was busy in the front seat, making one of the Native crafts that she sold up on the Danforth, leaned out of the front window and wagged a finger at her son.

"Don't you think I want you in school? It's that terrible teacher — she doesn't appreciate you at all. She doesn't know how smart you are. She thinks you're just a useless street kid and have no manners. As if I didn't teach you myself! Besides, she doesn't respect our Native customs."

Hawk stopped in his tracks, poised over an oily puddle. A slender boy, of average height, but wiry and strong, he fingered his long ponytail of blond hair and stared at his mother with his deep blue eyes. With his blandest, most innocent smile, he informed her, "Mrs. MacWhinney says you're not a Native at all, Ma. I heard her talking to another teacher. She says you're deluded. That you ought to be locked up. She says you're a pain in the neck."

His mother took the bait at once. She gave a yelp, as if someone had slapped her, and started screaming. "That plumped-up pea goose! That played-out pea-brained word-drudge! I'll have the old piss-pot fired! I'll push her off a high bridge. And I'll tell her so to her face — tomorrow morning!"

Mrs. Wilson — for although she called herself Storm Cloud, Hawk's mother's real name was Ruby Wilson — jumped out of the car, slapped at her buckskin skirt, and gave a pretty good imitation of a war cry.

"She'll take you back and treat you properly, or I'll know the reason why!" declared his mother. "The School Board respects me. They don't treat me like dirt. We've got tests to prove how smart you are. You didn't get all that from your father. You watch, you'll be back in class any time you want to be."

"And you won't pull me out of class if Mrs. MacWhinney treats me wrong? You'll let me fight my own battles?"

His mother gave him a sharp look and shook her head.

"I'm your mother," she reminded him. "I have a right to interfere any time I want. And it's not interference. It's just looking after your rights."

Hawk sighed and threw a stone rather hard into a puddle. Mrs. MacWhinney, his teacher, was an ex-librarian, and spent many days praising the virtues of good books, although she never once read her class a story. A sallow-faced woman with thin, gold-rimmed glasses and dark, empty eyes, she had a cultivated voice and prided herself on being a PhD graduate of some big western university. Maybe because of that she talked a lot, obviously enjoying the sound of her own voice. She didn't much like to be interrupted either. Now Hawk was imagining the terrific shouting match that would take place when his mother hauled him back to the school and she and his teacher began to up the ante with each other. The windows would rattle, the roof would shake, it would be embarrassing as hell. All the kids would giggle behind their hands and stare. They'd whisper, make fun of him, calling him names, and chase him around the playground later, and the teacher would feel justified and totally virtuous when she treated him in an even snootier way than before.

Mrs. MacWhinney obviously didn't believe the test results that showed that Hawk was quite a smart kid, smart enough even to get into the gifted class. Several times she had handed back his written work with a sour smile and called his attention to the large letter *P* that was written across the top of the first sheet.

"You know what that means, don't you?" she asked, pointing to her scrawl.

"*P* for perfect?" he beamed at her.

"Certainly not! It's a letter I reserve for very doubtful cases. For children who do POOR work and are a PROBLEM. It's a warning, it's the handwriting on the wall, telling a student that he or she simply MUST improve."

The first time she told him this, Hawk had simply shrugged his shoulders. The second time he said to her, "That work is much better than last time. Maybe the *P* should be smaller."

"I'll be the judge of that," she snapped.

"That's the problem," he complained, and was immediately sent off to the principal's office for being insolent.

Storm Cloud had hurried over to the school. She shook her head disapprovingly at Hawk, but demanded that the principal move her son to the Gifted Grade Four.

The principal, a well-dressed woman with perfect makeup and an artificial smile to match, leaned across her desk.

"But your son can't write two coherent sentences," she explained. "He can't spell, and he never finishes his work. And when he gets frustrated he throws things on the floor and then spits at the other students if they laugh at him."

"He's essentially verbal, that's why," his mother insisted. "It's part of our heritage, a tribal kind of thing. That teacher of yours should teach him to write! Or doesn't she know how? And, besides, when he seems to be spitting he's really just sharing his spiritual essence with the other children. It's a part of our culture you don't understand."

"For your information, Mrs. Wilson, I've always gotten high ratings in my 'sensitivity to minorities' scores. You may be sure that your son will receive fair treatment under this roof. I'm just trying to get your co-operation as we plan his future together."

"Watch out, Mum, the white lady wants you to sign a treaty," Hawk had joked, not very appropriately, perhaps. He was banished from the discussion then and there.

His memories of school, as you see, were not so great, but as he stomped around the vacant lot in the rain, circling the Oldsmobile and his mother, splashing in the puddles and throwing stones at the old tires and the hulking machinery, he still had a kind of itch to get back to that horrible class.

After all, despite the teacher's endless *P* ratings, he knew he was learning a few things, at least from the other students. There were books to read and kids who didn't always make fun of him, and who had neat things like iPods and cellphones with cameras and games and keyboards that they would sometimes let him try out.

Hawk jumped across a very large puddle and approached his mother, who had been thinking deep thoughts while he roamed through the back lot remembering some of his worst school moments.

Storm Cloud smiled at him, stepped over to the Oldsmobile, swung open one rusting door, picked up the tiny moccasins she'd been fashioning out of leather and fur and stowed them in a small box in front of the back seat. Then she took Hawk by the hand and led him slowly across the yard.

"I've got a plan," she said. "One that will solve most of our problems, I hope. I'm going to get you transferred to the gifted class."

"Mum, you must have been dreaming in Technicolor," he told her. "You already know that won't wash."

"Don't doubt me, son. I know what I'm doing. I want you to go over to Mr. Rizzuto's store — I don't care if it's raining — he's always happy to talk baseball, and he'll be glad to see you. Meanwhile, I'll just drop in on your father and the two of us will head over to the board and arrange for your transfer. It might take a few days, but it will be worth waiting for. I've heard about a couple of great teachers who might just be the ones to teach you properly and get you settled into school at last. That's what we want, isn't it?"

"I guess so."

"All right then. Let's lock up the car and get going. I can finish my work later. You okay walking to Rizzuto's without me?"

"Yeah, sure, Mum."

"All right, but you keep out of sight of that Rippers gang. They don't only prowl by night, you know. You remember how upset you were when they attacked you and stole your hat and baseball glove and ball on your way back from Mr. Rizzuto's store last month?"

Hawk winced, frowned, and bit his lip. "How could I forget it?"

His mother gave him a hug, pressing him close.

"Sorry, dear, to mention it, but it's a wonder they didn't murder you! The police never did a thing either. Too busy protecting rich white guys, I guess. Watch out for that gang, son, and don't talk to any strangers."

A few minutes later Hawk was walking down to the end of Hilbert Street, the street he and his mother called home, toward one of the busy thoroughfares that connected the north and south areas of the neighbourhood known as Riverdale.

He'd hated to be reminded by his mother of his stolen ball, cap, and first baseman's glove. It was a perfect one, that glove, almost broken in, and complete with the great Justin Morneau's signature stamped on it. It had been a present from his father, and after he practised awhile with that beauty, he was sure he'd make one of the neighbourhood teams, and maybe even play in the Little League. But now he knew he'd never see that glove again.

Silently, he cursed the gang that had ruined his future. The Rippers, they called themselves, and with good reason, for they were a street clan that specialized in harassing and fleecing younger kids. They liked to stalk ten- to twelve-year-olds — whom they'd threaten or even beat up, and then steal their techno-toys and sports equipment. The Rippers weren't choosy. They loved money, but depending on the quality of the merchandise, they were happy to steal almost anything, from iPods and watches to running shoes and Swiss Army knives.

Hawk shuddered and looked nervously around as he walked, for in his mind he could still see the gang's sneering faces. Haggard-looking and mean they were, those kids, a smelly, scary bunch who didn't care whether their victims were white, black, Native, or Asian, so long as the haul was worth the risk of getting nicked by the cops.

One of the gang he remembered most clearly was a boy they called Ringo — a short, nasty teen with a head like a turnip, all shaved, and wearing sunglasses taped on at the ears. A kid with thick arms covered with tattoos, Ringo had a soft, cooing voice that Hawk found disturbing. He had slipped Hawk's treasured glove out of his hand, stroked the leather gently and smiled at him, then suddenly shoved the glove as hard as he could into Hawk's face. So, with a burgeoning black eye and without his precious glove, Hawk had crept back home. After that, he'd had a few nightmares about Ringo.

But just then, looking around in every direction, he couldn't see any sign of that nasty gang, so he walked on bravely, heading straight for Mr. Rizzuto's store as his mother had told him to do.

Chapter 2

Holy Cow!

The drizzle was letting up a little. Hawk straightened up his shoulders and crossed the main thoroughfare, unbuttoning the top of his short poncho. Passersby, occupied with their own thoughts, hardly gave the boy a glance. Cars zoomed up and down the side streets, trucks with their lights flashing and warning beepers sounding backed into driveways to unload. Hawk dodged around a couple of women with prams, old men walking their dogs, and high-school girls busy on their cellphones. He looked away as he passed a police car parked outside a coffee shop — he was always afraid some cop would ask him why he wasn't in school, but there were other kids of various shapes and sizes on the street, and nobody paid him any attention.

Mr. Rizzuto's store was in the middle of a busy street on the edge of Chinatown, a colourful street lined with restaurants, grocery stores, fruit and flower stands, a magazine shop, and a tae kwon do place. Hawk knew that Mr. Rizzuto was quite well off. He had a fine house across the city, in Little Italy, a car even bigger, and in a lot better shape, than the wreck of an Oldsmobile that Storm Cloud and Hawk slept in. He also had a house in Riverdale, convenient to his shoe shop, an assistant he paid to do most of the shoe repair, and he possessed, with some of his cronies, season tickets to the home games of the Toronto Blue Jays.

This investment in baseball gave Mr. Rizzuto a great deal of joy, but it was also the source of his deepest unhappiness. Much as he liked the Blue Jays, his favourite team, the team of his childhood dreams, was the New York Yankees. Despite this, it had been years since he had visited the old Yankee Stadium, and he was very unlikely to visit the new one. That was surprising, because he was distantly related to the great Phil Rizzuto, Yankee all-star shortstop of the 1940s and 1950s. As a child, Mr. Rizzuto had often been taken to the stadium to see "Scooter" Rizzuto play on those famous championship Yankee teams that included Joe DiMaggio, Yogi Berra, and other Hall of Fame legends. But later in life he couldn't bring himself ever to return to that renowned ball park.

This was because — as he had often explained to Hawk — he was at odds with his only daughter, now a grown woman, who lived in New York. She was very successful in the fashion business and had a fine apartment on the Upper West Side, but she refused to have anything to do with her father. It seems he had offended her by disapproving, in no uncertain terms, of her fiancé, the man she loved. The couple had broken up years before as a result of her father's interference, and she had never married, for which she blamed Mr. Rizzuto. Over the years she had avoided him — she wouldn't even answer his emails, never mind take his phone calls or see him in person.

"I can't go to that city anymore," he told Hawk. "It makes me too sad. I can't enjoy baseball there — or anything. Just think! Me, a relative of the great Rizzuto, and I can't even visit that place. Sure, I can go sit in the park they named after him in New Jersey, but I just haven't got the heart to go anywhere near my Angelica. It's the sadness of my life."

Hawk felt a lot of sympathy for Mr. Rizzuto, but he didn't really understand the problem. It was like a lot of things with grownups — they seemed to tie themselves into knots when they didn't have to. He knew how bad he'd feel if his mother moved away and wouldn't talk to him — ever. But then he was a kid, and he needed his mum. If he was a grown-up like Mr. Rizzuto, and didn't have to live in a broken-down taxi, and had two houses, a store, a nice car, and tickets to all the Blue Jays games, he didn't think he'd feel so bad.

Hawk glanced up at the dingy old sign that said RIZZUTO SHOES REPAIR, pressed his face against the window pane, and tried to see who was inside. He caught a glimpse of Chick, the old man's sturdy assistant, working away at a bench behind the counter at what looked like a leather-stitching job. Chick usually wore a T-shirt with the Rizzuto number 10 on it to please his boss, but Hawk couldn't see much through the smeared glass. He pulled back, rubbing his wet cheeks with the top of his slimy poncho.

At that moment a bike bell rang behind him. He jumped as a girl's voice shouted his name.

"Hawk! How are you doing, bird-boy? Going to get your shoes fixed at last?"

A blue bicycle zoomed up and braked so suddenly that Hawk thought the bright red panniers would fly off the back and the rider might follow them in an arc through the shoe-store window.

She managed the stop very well, however, and seconds later she turned to him, a slender Asian girl with dark eyes, a bright smile, and a manner that seemed eager, almost restless, even though she was standing quite still.

Hawk saw that she was busying herself with a white fluffy thing that squirmed and whimpered in the bike's front basket.

"It's okay, Chew-Boy," she said, patting the very small dog that seemed a bit taken aback by the jolting stop. "We'll be home in a few minutes. Just giving him a ride," she told Hawk. "He misses me sometimes."

"I'm Panny Chang," she explained. "I saw you in the Rawson playground. Your shoes were worn out, and you fell and lost a sole. I notice you've got new ones, though."

Hawk remembered barging into a bunch of kids from the gifted class when he was playing dodge ball during lunch break a few weeks before. He'd crashed down against some tree roots in a far corner of the yard and lost a shoe, but instead of getting angry and shouting at him, the nerds just made a few witty jokes, tossed him his damaged shoe, and went back to some complicated game they were playing with cardboard origami figures.

"Have you been at school recently?" Panny asked. (Hawk had heard that she got her nickname because of the colourful panniers she sported on her bike.) "Somebody in your class said you were living in a taxicab. I didn't believe that, though."

"Believe it," Hawk said. "It's not too bad, really. Except on rainy days like this. I'm not in school now. Mrs. MacWhinney hates me and my mother wants to push her off a bridge. I want to get back to school, though. My mum's trying to get me into gifted."

"Good ambition! With all the other nuts, right? Anyway, we have two great teachers for our class. Ms. Calloway and Ms. Clark — you'll love them. They're strict but really cool. They know a lot and give us great projects. I'm doing one on China and Europe in the Middle Ages. We're doing a media study and a musical on *The Canterbury Tales.* But why are you hanging around this shoe store? Do you live around here?"

"No, I just live a few blocks away, behind the Shalimar Restaurant. The guy who owns this shoe store is a friend of mine. He likes baseball and coaches me. I'm going to be a baseball player — maybe. I might be a scientist, too — in case I don't make it in baseball."

Panny stood with her bike, petting Chew-Boy with one hand and steadying her handlebars with the other. Her yellow running shoes restlessly tapped the pavement as if she were about to take off.

"I like science, too," Panny told him. "Luckily, I'm good at math, but I think I might be a vet, or maybe a ballet dancer. There are quite a few options. I live down this street, by the way."

"Oh, yeah? Have you ever heard of a gang called the Rippers? They stole my best baseball stuff and gave me a black eye. I hope you don't run into them."

Panny's dark eyes grew wider. "That's terrible! Was it at night? Did they attack your taxicab? My parents don't let me go around at night. They don't attack people in the daytime, do they?"

"I don't think so. But you'd better be careful. That's a nice-looking bike and Chew-Boy wouldn't be much protection."

"Don't insult Chew-Boy — he's very smart. He can bite if he has to. But did you try to find the gang and get your stuff back?"

Hawk shook his head. "That would be crazy! I don't want to end up dead!"

Panny nodded. "I see your point. But maybe not direct action. Maybe just do some tracking and then turn them over to the police. Let me think about it. I have lots of friends in this neighbourhood. I can find out things. Maybe I'll see you in class in a few days — if you make it there. And just in case, I'll give you my cellphone number. You can call me if you have some big problem — but not *too* big a problem!"

Hawk was dumbfounded. He stood by as she wrote down the number. Was she serious in thinking she could do something? He could only nod, gape at her, and mumble, "Yeah, I'll see you … if I make that class…. And thanks for the number!" Panny smiled, waved, and wobbled away on her bike. She picked up speed quickly and zoomed off down the street.

Hawk, scratching his head and wondering about this unexpected encounter, turned and pushed open the door of the shoe shop.

Chick Ciccarelli, Mr. Rizzuto's assistant, glanced up from his workbench. He grunted and greeted Hawk with an ironical but friendly smile. "Well, well, look who's here!" He turned toward the back of the shop, the number 10 now clearly visible on his T-shirt. "Hey, Mr. Billy, it's the rookie, all by himself and looking wet." Hawk stood there awkwardly, suddenly feeling shy.

Ciccarelli stretched his muscular arms and yawned. "What's the matter, kid, they haul away your taxicab?"

Hawk started to answer, but before he could finish a sentence, a short, skinny old man darted out from the rear of the shop. He pulled off his straw boater, scratched his bushy grey hair and his long red nose, and beamed at the visitor.

"Hawk! Holy cow! Imagine that you show up now, and in the rain, too. I'm glad you're here, kid. I'm very glad. You and I have something big to talk over. C'mon in the back and I'll warm up a pizza — you look like you haven't had a decent lunch."

Chick Ciccarelli stood up and muttered, "Yeah, come to think of it, it's time for my break."

Hawk followed Mr. Rizzuto in to the back of the shop.

Chapter 3

The Bambino's Shadow

Mr. Rizzuto cut the pizza, lifted a generous slice onto a plate, and handed it to Hawk. It was delicious — thin crust, great tomato sauce, three cheeses, black olives, shrimp bigger than a wrestler's thumb, and small chunks of pineapple. Mr. Rizzuto drank red wine and passed a large glass of lemonade over to Hawk.

"Listen, kid, this is crazy. You showing up here and me making the biggest discovery of my life. What are you doing in these parts in the rain anyway? We can't play stickball. Don't tell me they junked your taxi?"

Hawk swallowed a large mouthful of pizza and explained. "No, not that. It's that my mum's on the warpath. She's off to see my dad. She wants to get him to go to the School Board with her so they can get me into another class. My teacher's an old witch."

"Oh, oh, you talk like that about your teacher? Wow! Times have changed. So your mum wants you to transfer to another class, I get it. Probably a good idea.... By the way, did you ever hear anything more on that stuff the Rippers stole from you? I've been meaning to look into that. Only trouble is, I don't like to go to the police. Not that I ever have any trouble with them. It's just that some of my family wouldn't appreciate it if I run to the police with every little problem. We like to take care of our own business."

"That's okay, Mr. Rizzuto. I just met a girl from my school on the street out there. A Chinese girl. She knows this neighbourhood and she's going to help me find the gang and turn them over to the police. I don't think it will happen, though."

"You never know, kid, you never know. I hope that girl isn't heading for trouble. I'm going to do some checking myself. I have some connections, and not only in the neighbourhood. But what's this about your mum and dad — don't tell me they're getting together again."

Hawk shook his head sadly. "No, I don't think so. It's just this once, to help me."

"Okay. But if you don't mind me asking, whatever happened between them? I know you gave me a rundown once before, but now that you and I are going to be partners.... If I remember correctly, you're still on good terms with your dad, right?"

Hawk picked up on the surprising sentence at once. "You and I are going to be partners?" he said, and stared wide-eyed at Mr. Rizzuto.

"I hope so, but first tell me about your mum and dad. Is she finally going to accept some help from him?"

"Only so I can change classes. My dad's still fed up with my mum. As you know, he's a full-blooded Ojibway-Cree and he works for the Native Centre, and my mum pretends that she's a Native, too. She's always trying to outdo him, and telling him how he should act. She thinks he doesn't like her because her parents came from Scotland and she's not a Native at all. So she tries to be more of a Native than he is and that drives my dad crazy."

Mr. Rizzuto nodded sagely. "Sure, I understand. She wants to be more Catholic than the Pope."

Hawk shrugged his shoulders and looked baffled. He took a slug of the lemonade.

"My mum takes care of me. She tries pretty hard, but things don't always come out right. It's not really her fault — at least sometimes it's not. We don't have much money and she can't afford an apartment. The taxi's okay. But the people from Welfare don't like it."

"I sure hope not. Maybe they'll find you something, huh? Maybe I'll find you something better."

Hawk swallowed hard and posed the question. "Did you say something about us being partners, Mr. Rizzuto?"

"I sure hope so. But I have to explain. You know, because I got some money saved up, some property and things, people think I can do what I want. Yeah sure, I'm comfortable. I can buy this little thing or that, up to a point, but some things you can't buy, you have to go out and find them, or earn them somehow. Some of the best things are like that. You know what I mean?"

Hawk frowned. "You mean like me being a baseball player, or you getting your daughter to like you?"

Mr. Rizzuto winced, then nodded gravely at the boy. "Yeah, you're a smart kid all right. You know what I mean.... But I'll tell you something else. Then you'll see where I'm coming from. Think about this. You know how sometimes you know something, but really you don't know it, because you never really took it out of your mind and looked at it, dusted it off, and took it on in a real way. It was just a thought, bumping around in your brain with lots of other ideas, then one day, bingo! It's real and you're ready to deal with it."

Hawk gave him a puzzled look — what was the old man going on about? He frowned a deeper frown, gulped a bit more lemonade, and tried to zoom in. "You mean, like my mum — she talked about getting me into gifted, but she really didn't do anything about it. It was just a thought. Now she's off trying to make it happen."

Mr. Rizzuto sprang out of his chair so quickly it made Hawk choke. "You got it! That's it! That's exactly what happened in my case — between me and Babe Ruth!"

For a few seconds Hawk was quite speechless. Of course he knew who Babe Ruth was — probably the greatest baseball player of them all, or at least the most famous, not to mention the greatest Yankee star. All the same, the boy was puzzled. He put his glass down, leaned over and started to ask a question. Mr. Rizzuto, however, whose boater had fallen off (he wore it everywhere, inside and out, even in winter), and whose impressive nose had turned a brighter red, quickly circled the table, stopped, and pulled a folded sheet of paper from his pocket.

"Here, kid, take a gander at this!"

Hawk — as his principal had pointed out — wasn't much of a writer, but he could read like a demon. Slowly, he unfolded the paper and read the story printed there, one that had obviously been downloaded from a computer site.

Babe Ruth's First Home Run

Out in Lake Ontario lie the Toronto islands, which also have an interesting history.... At Hanlan's Point (named after Ned Hanlan, an international rowing star) there was once an amusement park and a small stadium, home of the minor league Toronto Maple Leaf baseball team. There, in 1914, a 19-year-old pitcher named Babe Ruth, playing for the visiting Providence Rhode Island Grays, hit his first professional home run. It's believed the ball is still in the lake.

Hawk lowered the paper slowly and stared at Mr. Rizzuto. "Gosh, I didn't know Babe Ruth played in Toronto. I didn't even know he was a pitcher. Too bad the ball was lost in the lake. I guess it would be pretty valuable now, wouldn't it?"

Mr. Rizzuto took a step and a jump, startling the boy as he grabbed him and began thumping on the shoulders. "Kid! You're a genius! Your mother is quite right! Of course the ball would be worth a fortune, maybe a million dollars even! Not only that, but whoever found it would be famous. It would be like finding Blackbeard's treasure or that cup they call the Holy Grail — whatever that is! It would be a life adventure, kid, a real life adventure!"

Hawk stepped back and shook his head doubtfully. "Sure, I get you, Mr. Rizzuto, but the ball's lost. This article says it went into the lake, and by now it would just be a few soggy pieces of string, or whatever those old baseballs were made of."

"String and cork and horsehide, kid, string and cork and horsehide. A few years before 1914 the Spalding Company that made the baseballs substituted cork for rubber in the centre of the ball, so guys began hitting more home runs. If that ball still exists it would look something like today's baseballs, only the seams would be flat, not raised. And you know what? I think it may still exist."

Hawk shook his head. "Oh, come on, Mr. Rizzuto. It says right here in the article that the ball probably went into the lake. If it didn't get ruined, if it still existed, somebody would have found it by now."

Mr. Rizzuto paced back and forth across the room, his hands waving as if he were directing traffic or conducting an orchestra. "Not necessarily! There's no proof at all that the ball's in the lake. Did you ever watch those games in San Francisco where Barry Bonds would hit home runs out of the park and into the bay? You remember what happened then?"

Hawk scratched his head. He hadn't had a chance to watch TV very regularly, but he had a vague recollection of a store window with several TVs flashing out sports scenes to lure the customers. He remembered a swing and a ball clearing the stands and a water scene with boats, kayaks, canoes — all kinds of small craft — darting like insects to reach a tiny object smacked by the potent Bonds bat into San Francisco Bay.

"You mean somebody could have picked the ball up — fetched it out of the water?"

"Sure, why not? It's a fun thing to do. And remember, Toronto Harbour was full of small craft, even in those days. And there was an amusement park on the island, right next to the stadium. Just think of it, kid. There would be lots of folks playing around there, lots of people on the shore, and kids swimming in the lake, boys scooting around on bikes and playing catch. They would hear the roar of the crowd — there was probably a pretty good crowd watching the game — and the folks outside would see this ball come sailing out of the stadium. Don't you think some smart kid, or somebody in a boat, would have grabbed that ball as a souvenir?

They wouldn't have just let it sink in the lake, any more than the folks outside of Candlestick Park in San Francisco would."

Hawk stared at Mr. Rizzuto. "Wow! I think you've got a point!" He thought for a minute, then added, "But once Babe Ruth became famous, wouldn't they have brought that ball out and put it on the market? If somebody had it, it would have been identified and checked out long ago."

Mr. Rizzuto shook his head. "No way! Think about it. Nobody knew who Babe Ruth was then. He was just a kid pitcher who hit a home run. This was just a baseball they found outside a small-time ballpark, or fished out of the lake just for fun. Nobody would have bothered to find out who hit the ball. It would have ended up in somebody's toy box or rec room — if they had rec rooms in those days. It would have ended up in a box in somebody's attic. And that's where it probably is, right now. And I'm telling you, we're going to find that box! And it's going to make us a lot of money and get us a lot of attention on TV and in the newspapers! That is, if you believe me, my young friend, Hawk, if you want to help me look for it. As I said, I think we should be partners. We should look for this famous baseball together."

"Wow!"

Hawk was amazed at his friend's offer, and at Mr. Rizzuto's obvious enthusiasm. At the same time, a small voice whispered in the boy's inner ear: *This is crazy. This is never going to happen. That ball has been lost forever, and we certainly aren't going to find it after all these years.*

Mr. Rizzuto looked at him and seemed to read his thoughts, to pick up right away on his doubts. "I know you're excited, but I see a little tiny gleam of doubt in those eyes of yours, kid, and I don't blame you. It all seems pretty much like a pipe dream, I know, the pipe dream of an old Yankee fan and a relative of that great Yankee player, Scooter Rizzuto. But let me fill you in on my plans. I'm not dreaming, I'm not handing you a line of bull, I really do have an idea that we can find that ball. Let's sit down at the table here and I'll explain."

Mr. Rizzuto lifted the empty plates off the table and carried them over to the sink in the corner of the room. He poured more lemonade for Hawk, sat down, and began to talk.

"Okay, kid. Here's my plan. See if you think I'm nuts or just some old guy raving. Let's assume that the Babe Ruth ball was picked up by someone. Let's assume it was kept as a souvenir. Now, we can't prove that either of these things happened, but the there's no reason why they *couldn't* have happened. Now, I've checked out all the guys I could find who really know something about this city, about Toronto's history. And I've looked for a guy who isn't just an old-fashioned bookworm expert, but somebody who has the technology to make things happen fast.

"And guess what? I found a guy. His name is Dr. Wingate, and he's a retired history professor who has got everything about this city's history on his computer. All the famous buildings and sites, he's got a set of files on them — *big files.* He's been feeding information into those files for years. You want to know something about the old St. Lawrence Market, or the Broadview House Hotel, or Casa Loma, well, this guy's got all the dope.

"So, guess what? I've hired him to research the old ballpark for me. I've hired him to give me a complete picture of the place in 1914. He's checking that, and, in fact, he's looking at the whole of Hanlan's Point. Before long, we'll know everything there is to know about the place — what went on there, what kind of folks went to the old amusement park and the baseball stadium, who hung around there and had maybe a business or a concession on the beach. In other words, *who might have picked up that baseball!*"

Hawk swallowed his lemonade, nearly choking on it — he was very excited. "That sounds great, Mr. Rizzuto. But you haven't heard anything yet, right?"

"Nothing yet, but it's early. The main thing is, this smart guy, Dr. Wingate, didn't think I was nuts. He thought it might be a long shot, but that he just might turn up something. You see, he'd read the same article in the *Sun* that I read. It was about a month ago, and they mentioned the whole Babe Ruth lost baseball thing. Of course I'd heard that story before, but I never thought of chasing after that ball. It's like I said, sometimes you know something but it doesn't hit you in the face. You know it, but you don't think of doing anything about what you know. Well, when I read that article, it was like I was struck by lightning. I just knew I had to find that baseball!"

"So when will you hear from Dr. Wingate?"

Mr. Rizzuto scratched his head. "I don't know. Pretty soon, I hope. There's one thing, though, one thing that worries me. When I went to this guy, he listened to me, looked at me kind of funny, then, as I was leaving, he clued me in to something that didn't exactly make me dance for joy."

"What was that?"

"He said somebody else had asked him for exactly the same information. That it wouldn't take him long to put my package together, because he was already working on it."

"Wow! I wonder who else is after that baseball."

"He wouldn't tell me. Professional discretion — that's what he called it. I couldn't get even a hint from him."

Hawk thought for a minute. "Could it be a collector — somebody who collects autographs and stuff, or baseball cards? Maybe even somebody from the States, or from the Baseball Hall of Fame? Somebody like that?"

"Sure. It could be anybody. You know, kid, there are a lot of angles to this. There are a whole lot of collectors out there. Then there are also a whole lot of forgers and guys who peddle counterfeit stuff. They make money from their swindles so they can afford big prices to buy real authentic stuff. Then they sell that good stuff for even more money. So they get rich both ways. It's a tough world out there, I tell you. But you and I are going to beat it."

"So we really are partners, Mr. Rizzuto? And if we find the ball and make money you're going to cut me in?"

"Of course! But you're going to earn your share. There may be errands to run, things you can help me with so I can spend more time checking out things with Mr. Wingate. And I'm hoping that if we do cash in on this you can use some of the money for a good purpose. Maybe for your education, and right away to find you a much better place to live."

Hawk nodded. The day had started out being boring, but had gotten much better! He couldn't wait to get back to tell his mother. Even starting out in a new class seemed pretty ordinary compared to this. This was a treasure hunt, this was adventure, the kind of thing he'd dreamed about but never thought would happen. He left Mr. Rizzuto's as soon as he could and make a beeline for his home in the taxi.

Chapter 4

Suspicion

"Babe Ruth's baseball? It sounds like a wild goose chase to me," his mother said when he told her about Mr. Rizzuto's idea. But seeing his disappointment, she added quickly, "No harm in it, though, I suppose, provided you keep your mind on your schoolwork and your new class. I just hope that father of yours goes to the board again tomorrow, as he promised."

Hawk frowned and nodded. It was a damp evening, but Selim, the restaurant manager, had sent out a small heater and a power pack, so the inside of the taxi was warm and almost cozy. Hawk used a flashlight to read the sports magazine his father had sent over for him, while his mother worked on one of her "Native" craft projects. After a while, he felt sleepy, the magazine print and pictures began to blur — minute by minute he nodded off, and soon was fast asleep.

Bright sunlight woke Hawk. He stirred, blinked, yawned twice, and crawled out of the taxi. His mother was still fast asleep, curled up on the front seat. He crossed the yard, stepping around the puddles, creeping past the trash cans and the Dumpsters, and stepping inside Selim's building on his way to the washroom. A few minutes later, his face scrubbed and shining, he slipped on his jacket and headed across town toward the practice lot.

It looked like a great day for baseball and he knew that Mr. Rizzuto and the boys would be there. Hawk always loved the baseball practice, even though most of the other guys were better players than he was. Martin Schiller was strong, and a terrific hitter. The Contreras boys, who made fun of everything, did acrobatic catches and slid into bases like the pros. They, along with Hawk, were the regulars, but other kids turned up too, depending on who Mr. Rizzuto decided to coach that day. There was a skinny, freckle-faced, redheaded kid who wanted to be a pitcher; an overweight Chilean boy who always arrived wearing a catcher's mask; and two sisters with matching ponytails who could run like the wind. The sisters were unusual among the baseball gang, for they always headed off to school after the practice. Most of Mr. Rizzuto's ballplayers, in one way or another, managed to avoid regular classes.

The tiny lot Mr. Rizzuto had set up was close to the railroad tracks in South Riverdale. None of the kids knew whether he owned or rented it. Perhaps he had done a trade with some other businessman or developer, but once or twice a week he would turn up with a van and all the necessary equipment. The playing field would be spruced up, any kids already there would be invited to take part, and the practice would begin.

Mr. Rizzuto's idea was to train kids so that they could get entry to the Major Division of the Little League, which was mostly for eleven- or twelve-year-olds. Some of the kids, like the Contreras boys, could easily have made it, but they liked training with Mr. Rizzuto, who knew a lot about baseball and was very generous with his time and money. Alex and Pedro Contreras were the sons of a Cuban diplomat. They were supposedly being home-schooled and had lots of freedom. In fact, they spent most of it playing computer games, so their father insisted they do outdoor stuff as well, so they trained regularly with Mr. Rizzuto. Martin Schiller, who was from Kitchener, lived with his aunt, but she drank a lot, so he could duck school and had lots of free time. (His mother and father had been killed in a car crash.) Most of the other kids also had some problems.

Hawk was there because, the year before, he hadn't made the Little League team he'd tried out for. It was a junior team, but even so, he couldn't seem to hit or field anything that day, and at the same time the kids had a good laugh at his ragged clothes and his long blond hair. He felt scared, out of place, terrible — and after a short session that seemed to go on forever, the coach patted him on the head and told him he "just wasn't ready."

Mr. Rizzuto, who was watching the tryouts that day, stepped over and invited Hawk to join his practice sessions. When Hawk started out with Mr. Rizzuto, though, the Contreras brothers, who'd heard about his failure, kidded him unmercifully. "How come a blond Native is playing baseball?" Pedro asked. "He must want to sign up with the Cleveland Indians," his brother answered. "What about the Atlanta Braves?" Pedro added with a snicker.

But Mr. Rizzuto finally shut them up. "There have been plenty of full-blooded Native big leaguers, of all shapes and sizes," he told the boys, though he could only name a few. "Rudy York, Allie Reynolds, and Joba Chamberlain," he said, and then hesitated. "And a lot more with some Native blood in their veins," he added gruffly. "Just like Hawk."

After that, Martin Schiller and a couple of other kids who came only once in a while treated Hawk much better. And slowly, session by session, he made some progress in his batting and fielding.

On this day Hawk was particularly eager to get to the practice lot. If he was going to be a millionaire, he hoped it would happen quickly! And maybe Mr. Rizzuto had already found out something about the Babe's baseball. Hawk ran the last half-block to the field, past the warehouses, sheds, and rundown houses that ran along the edge of the railway line. From a few blocks away he spotted the big red equipment van, then, as he came closer, he saw the gang in the lot. Mr. Rizzuto, wearing his Yankees cap, was hitting fly balls to the kids. The two ponytailed girls, in Blue Jays caps and shirts, waved and shouted "Hawk!" Martin Schiller nodded to him. The Chilean kid, who was wearing his catcher's mask as usual, kicked at the stones, and Alex Contreras shouted from a distance, "Hey, kid! You comin' over from T-ball?"

Hawk ignored the insult (T-ball was for really young kids), and ran to pick up one of the gloves that were stacked on a bench near the sidewalk. Then he noticed the newcomer, a dark-skinned kid in very old jeans and a ragged Florida Marlins jersey.

As Hawk ran up to the backstop, this kid jumped up from the grass to shag a long fly. He was a good fielder, it seemed, cruising back with ease, and reaching up at the last minute to snare the ball. Funny thing, though, Hawk noticed — it looked like the kid was using a first baseman's glove.

"That's Elroy Whittaker," Mr. Rizzuto explained as he welcomed Hawk to the field. "Help yourself to a glove and go join him."

Hawk selected his favourite glove from a pile on the bench and jogged out past the Contreras brothers and the ponytail girls. He couldn't help but envy Elroy his glove, one he must have brought with him, since Mr. Rizzuto hadn't provided any first basemen's gloves since Hawk's own glove was stolen by the Rippers.

When the next shot came arcing out it seemed to be Hawk's ball. "I got it!" he shouted, racing back at top speed, reaching up at the last minute to snare it. But the ball never touched his glove. A figure darted in front of him, a glove went up, and Elroy sped away with the baseball, hidden for a moment in the webbing of his big glove.

"Jerk-face! I called for it!" Hawk shouted. Elroy swung back, shrugged his shoulders and laughed. "You 'bout to miss it," he said.

"I didn't miss it," Hawk shouted. "You cut me off!"

Elroy trotted off and set himself several yards away, ready for the next shot.

"All right, Hawk, you take this one!" Mr. Rizzuto shouted, and hit a line drive in the boy's direction. It was tricky, a dying quail, and Hawk sprang forward, got a glove on it, but dropped the ball. Sheepishly, and thoroughly disgusted with himself, he picked it up and tossed it in toward the backstop.

Mr. Rizzuto handed the bat to Martin Schiller, who began hitting grounders to the Contreras boys and the two girls while the older man started trying out pitches with the Chilean boy. "Get down there — block it with your body," he shouted as a low fastball bounced past the young catcher.

Hawk and Elroy, idle for a moment, drifted warily together.

"Where'd you get the Marlins jersey?" Hawk asked, hardly looking at the tall boy, and really interested not in his ragged shirt but in the smooth, shining leather glove.

"Down in Jacksonville — that's where I come from. But my mom came up here, so I'm here for now."

"You go to school?"

"We didn't find no school yet. I might go pretty soon."

Unable to resist any longer, with odd thoughts percolating through his mind, Hawk asked, "Nice glove. Did you bring that with you too?"

Elroy looked away and shifted his feet nervously. "No, I bought it right here," he said. "Real cheap." Then, after a pause, "Wanna have a try?"

"Sure." Hawk reached out and accepted the other boy's glove. His hands were shaking — which he did his best to conceal — as he brought the glove close to have a look. He fingered it for a minute, cleared his throat, and said, "Justin Morneau signature. Good player. Born in Canada."

"Yeah? I didn't know that. It's a good glove, best I ever had."

Hawk held his breath as he turned the glove over. He was looking for a small red spot on the inside of the glove, under the thumb section. When he saw it, he swallowed hard, and without looking at Elroy, said in a low, controlled voice, "You bought this here? Where'd you get it? I might like to get one."

Elroy stepped back without answering. He didn't meet Hawk's gaze. Gently but firmly, he retrieved the glove, then started to walk away. "I didn't buy it. My mom got it — from a yard sale." He said this over his shoulder, without once looking back. Then he ran hard toward the backstop.

Hawk stood shivering in his tracks. *It was his glove, the one that the Rippers had stolen!* The tiny red mark on the thumb base had been made by an accidental spill from one of his mother's dyes — there was no mistaking it.

Confused, he stood in his tracks and watched the others. What should he do? Try to get the glove back from Elroy? Tell Mr. Rizzuto? He felt frightened, angry, a bit sick. It was his glove, but what would Elroy say if he challenged him? What would Mr. Rizzuto think? He was sure that the older man didn't know about the red spot. He never wore his glasses when he was playing or coaching, and Hawk had never mentioned that mark to him. Maybe Mr. Rizzuto would say that if Elroy's mother had bought the glove at a yard sale, even if it was stolen goods, it was his to keep. But Elroy had been nervous about the glove, saying first that he'd bought it, then claiming his mother had picked it up at a sale. Why would he change his story? Something funny was going on here.

Hawk drifted in toward the backstop and the other kids. The Contreras brothers were playing catch with the girls, Mr. Rizzuto was still pitching to the Chilean boy, and Elroy was standing behind the catcher to field the balls he missed.

Martin Schiller, however, was walking toward Hawk, looking as if something was on his mind. The stocky, dark-haired boy never had much to say, but when he came up to where Hawk was standing, he shot out a question. "So, did he show it to you?" he asked in a low voice, looking over his shoulder, although no one else was close by.

Hawk gaped at him. "You mean the glove? Yeah, he did." He paused and then started to add, "But you know something —"

"Yeah, it's your glove," Martin interrupted. "I recognized it right away when Elroy showed it to me — after he got here."

"Whew! So I'm not crazy! I was sure it was my glove.... Where did he tell you he got it?"

"He said he bought it on the street, real cheap — that a couple of kids practically gave it to him."

"Jeez! He changes his story every time. What am I going to do, Martin?"

"I don't know. I guess he wasn't one of those Rippers that lifted your glove?"

"Nah. They were all white kids. Nasty kids. Elroy doesn't seem like them — not exactly."

"He's got something to hide, though. If we ask him anything, he's going to clam up," Martin said. He thought for a moment, frowning and shifting his feet and staring at the ground, but when he spoke again his glance was sharp and pointed. "Why don't we follow him home and see who he hangs out with?"

Chapter 5

Spies in Motion

"We gotta be careful when we take off," Martin said. "Otherwise he'll spot us for sure."

Hawk shook his head doubtfully. "I've got a better idea. You've got a cellphone, don't you, Martin?"

"Sure — I've got it with me."

Hawk fumbled in one of his pockets and gave a tiny shout of joy when his fingers came out clutching a crumpled piece of paper. "Good, I thought I'd lost this! Here, call this number on your phone. If you get her, pass it to me."

Martin shrugged his shoulders and made the call. After a few seconds he handed the phone to Hawk. "You have to leave a message," he said.

"Yeah, she'll be at school." Hawk frowned and spoke into the phone. "Hi, Panny? This is Hawk, remember? I don't know if you're free, but if you are, could you meet me on the Danforth at Jones around three-thirty or four o'clock? We've got a lead on the Rippers gang. Somebody turned up with my baseball glove and we need to watch him. If you can make it, please come."

Hawk signed off and explained to Martin. "If you can follow him and see where he hangs out, I can meet Panny later and we can go and watch his place. If he's connected with the Rippers, we might find out."

"Sure, but I'll join you at four, too. I'll tell you what I found out and help you watch the guy. Three heads are better than two."

"Great! If you get there before me, look out for a Chinese girl with crazy panniers on her bike.... Now we'd better get back to playing ball."

They waved at Mr. Rizzuto and walked toward the backstop. For the next hour Hawk was caught up in the practice — fielding grounders, shagging flies, hitting Mr. Rizzuto's almost-curveball, trading insults with the Contreras boys, joking with the ponytail girls, waiting for the fat boy to take off his mask (he did it at least once during every session). All the time, Hawk secretly watched Elroy, and kept his eye on his stolen glove, wanting badly just to take it away from him, but realizing that he had to be patient, to find out if Elroy was part of the Rippers gang or just an innocent guy who had happened to get hold of a "hot" glove.

When at last the practice was over, Mr. Rizzuto took Hawk aside and, as they were loading the equipment into the van, winked at him and said, out of the hearing of the others, "No word yet, kid, but don't get impatient. Things are happening!"

Hawk knew he was talking about the lost Babe Ruth ball.

Soon Elroy departed, his glove tucked under his arm. Martin Schiller waited until he had drifted out of sight down the street and then took off in the same direction.

"You doing anything now, Hawk?" Mr. Rizzuto asked. "You can come back to the store, eat lunch, and help Chick out. I've got a few places to go. What time do you have to get home?"

Hawk pondered this, then told him, not quite truthfully, "Oh, I've got to meet my mother on the Danforth around three-thirty or four. I can walk over there from your store."

With the van in motion, Mr. Rizzuto began to give Hawk a few additional tips about how to improve his batting and fielding. "Don't get me wrong, kid," he said, when he had finished elaborating on his advice. "You're good enough right now to play senior Little League — I'd bet my store on it! But you may as well do a few more sessions with me before you try out again. We don't want to take any chances."

"Don't worry, I'll make it," Hawk assured him. "I'm gonna do okay in school, too."

Mr. Rizzuto deposited Hawk at the store, and after lunch Chick got him running errands. Hawk enjoyed cruising the mostly familiar streets, and he knew it would earn him a few dollars from Mr. Rizzuto. Nonetheless, the time passed slowly, and the afternoon dragged on. Anxious to get over to talk to Martin, and to find out if Panny would really help him, he left the store early, taking his time to walk up Jones to the Danforth.

As he drifted along (he didn't want to arrive *too* early) his thoughts shot from one disturbing idea to another. He imagined himself in a classroom with all the "smart" kids, trying to show them that he was just as smart as they were. But suppose he started muffing his reading, and completely messed up his math? The teachers would shake their heads in disapproval. He'd look like a fool!

These fears he managed to shove away as he began to think of how he would get his baseball glove back from Elroy. Sure, Elroy didn't seem like such a bad guy, but it was *his* glove and he wanted it back badly. Would he have to confront Elroy, fool him somehow, and steal the glove back? He had no idea. And what about that "treasure," the famous Babe Ruth baseball? Maybe that really was a pipe dream of Mr. Rizzuto's. Maybe he'd never escape from that taxicab, maybe nothing would work out and he'd be dragged away to some Children's Aid place where he'd never see his mum or dad again. All of a sudden he felt panicky, helpless, and very confused.

Hawk stopped in his tracks, and fighting back tears of frustration, swore out loud and spat into the street. An old lady passing by gave him a disapproving look and cackled sweetly, "Oh dear! How nasty! Why aren't you in school, little boy?"

He thumbed his nose at her, scurried away, broke into a jog, and was overjoyed when the bustling, down-to-earth Danforth hove into sight. His run seemed to blow all the negative thoughts out of his head.

Still, as he approached his destination, Hawk kept looking warily around, remembering that his mother often tried to peddle her street wares on the Danforth. He had chosen the Jones intersection, where she seldom hung out, but since he'd learned that you couldn't count on anything, and that things had a way of turning out weirdly, he kept his eyes peeled for her anyway.

The Danforth, busy as it was, and lined by stores, coffee shops, and restaurants, was not intimidating. The buildings weren't too high, the traffic was steady but not overwhelming, and the sidewalks were neither crowded nor deserted.

Hawk came out on the thoroughfare, looked left and right, and sure enough, spotted Panny on her bike (red panniers again today) across the street in front of a small corner coffee shop. And there, right beside her, was the reliable Martin, who spied Hawk at once and waved him over. Minutes later, Martin was spilling out his story.

"I followed him all right. It was a long walk. Lucky he didn't have a bike. A couple of times I thought he spotted me, but I guess not. He lives west of Pape down by Lake Shore Boulevard. It's on one of those side streets that point toward the lake, a small wooden house, a bit shabby, but not too bad. There's lots of warehouses, parked cars, and alleys near the place. It won't be too hard to stake it out."

Panny winked at Hawk. "Martin watches a lot of TV crime shows, can't you tell? He filled me in on what happened at your practice. I just hope Elroy's mother didn't really buy your glove at a yard sale! So let's keep our fingers crossed and head down there — it's a long way. I'll bike, and you guys take the bus. I'll meet you at Eastern and Pape, by the movie studios, and we'll check out this kid's house."

They met with no trouble, and a good half-hour later were set up down the street from a small wooden house with two entrances, squeezed between a faceless warehouse and a printer's showroom. The house, covered with old white siding, had a rickety porch and steps and a smear of rough grass that lined the sidewalk. Above the porch roof, a couple of small bay windows, overhung by pointed gables, showed their plain brown curtains. The curtains revealed nothing; the house seemed insignificant and out of place on that commercial street.

Hawk gaped at it, shook his head, and said wryly, "Well, it's not much of a place to live, but it's better than a taxi."

"Yeah, I can't wait to see that taxi of yours," Panny said. "I hope we don't have to hang around here too long. Somebody will get suspicious. Anyway, I brought a few snacks."

She pulled two apples, a couple of granola bars, and soft drinks for each of the boys from her panniers. Then they organized their watch on the house. Panny would ride around the streets a bit, so as not to attract attention. Meanwhile, Hawk and Martin settled down in an alley with a good view of the house — a large Dumpster fronted it and they could hide behind it if they had to take cover. Panny would come and let them know if she saw anyone who looked suspicious approaching the place. Both Panny and Martin had iPods with them, and from time to time Hawk borrowed Martin's.

Even so, time passed very slowly. Cars drove up and down the street, one or two people were visible in a nearby showroom window and a few more in a car lot, but there were no pedestrians — and not even a dog or a cat in sight.

"This is bleak," Hawk said. "I just hope the police don't cruise by and see us. They'll start asking questions if they do."

"We could take a walk, but someone in the house might spot us," Martin said. He yawned, sat down on the hard concrete of the alley, and handed his iPod to Hawk. After a while, Panny cycled past, giving them a covert wave, and saying, as if they hadn't noticed, "Nothing yet!"

More time passed and they watched, bored and restless, as the light moved slowly across the alley walls, though sunset was still far away. Just when they were beginning to wonder if they would see anyone at all, a woman appeared at the street corner and trudged along toward the house. She was a heavy-set black woman wearing sunglasses, who appeared to be hauling some groceries in her large shopping bag.

"Elroy's mother?" Martin whispered. Hawk shrugged his shoulders. But as the woman came up to the house and started to climb the rickety steps of one of the dwellings, Hawk whispered back, "It must be."

The boys crouched together, trying to make themselves invisible in the alley. The woman used her key and went into the house. Panny whizzed by on her bike, and told them, "Something will happen now!"

More time passed, but just when the boys had decided that Panny was wrong, the door of the house opened, and two kids came out.

"There's our Elroy," Martin said. "It's about time."

Hawk didn't answer. He was staring at the boys as they came down the steps, staring at them with wide eyes. Elroy was a good foot taller than his companion, but he looked a bit skinny and insignificant next to him. The other boy, short and stocky, wore old overalls and a tattered work shirt with rolled-up sleeves that revealed his heavily tattooed arms. Hatless, his eyes hidden behind big dark sunglasses, he pushed Elroy forward, smiling as he ushered him along the sidewalk.

Hawk recognized this second boy at once, but stood there, his hands beginning to tremble and his throat tightening until at last he got the words out: "Martin! That guy he's with, I know him. They call him Ringo, and he's the rat who stole my glove. You know what that means — Elroy must be one of the Rippers."

Chapter 6

Messages at Night

Martin shook his head in dismay. "Yeah? You sure? Well, that's bad news. Maybe we'd better get out of here."

"Okay, but ... wait." Hawk wanted to be sure the coast was clear and peered cautiously around the Dumpster. Then he stole forward to the end of the alley and cast a glance down the street.

"They've stopped at the corner," he told his friend. "Ugh! Ringo has an arm on Elroy's shoulder. They must be gang members together. I don't get it. I heard the Rippers don't like Afro kids."

"Maybe they're getting more broad-minded," Martin said.

"Hold it! Elroy's coming back. We have to hide again. I wonder how Panny's doing?"

They scurried back behind the Dumpster and

sprawled on the hard concrete, peering anxiously at the house across the street. A few seconds later Elroy reappeared. He stopped at the bottom of the steps and looked around. He didn't seem to be looking at anything in particular, but was apparently pondering something. Then he shrugged his shoulders and disappeared into the house.

A moment later, Panny zoomed into sight and braked sharply in front of the Dumpster. She cast a glance up and down the street, then slowly wheeled her bike into the alley.

"Wow! That was interesting. Who's that weirdo Elroy was with? Must be a Ripper for sure. He looks like an evil dwarf from a comic book."

"That's the guy who stole my glove and gave me a black eye," Hawk explained. "They call him Ringo — it's some kind of joke they have."

"I'm glad they have a sense of humour. They laughed while they beat you up, right?"

"It's horrible that Elroy's one of them. Not good for him and not good for getting my glove back. What do we do now? Maybe tell Mr. Rizzuto?"

"Wait a minute, you haven't heard everything," Panny said. "I was able to watch them quite closely. Just some dumb girl on a bike, they thought. And after watching them, I'm not so sure that your baseball pal Elroy is one of them at all."

"What? Why not? He had an arm around the guy. They looked like friends to me," Martin insisted.

"A spider hangs around with a fly, doesn't he?" Panny reminded him. "And they get close together in the web before the spider eats him for dinner. So what does an arm on the shoulder prove? I was watching Elroy's face, and trust me, that kid was scared to death. His hands were trembling the whole time. He looked a bit sick, too, when he started back for his mum's place over there."

"You mean that the Rippers are threatening Elroy? Then why did he get the glove from them?"

"Carrot and stick," Panny suggested. "It could be — we don't know for sure — that the gang is setting him up, or using him for something. They're rewarding him and drawing him into the web. Anyway, he didn't look very happy. If he's really a bad guy, he's not enjoying it very much."

"What do we do now?" Martin asked.

"We keep spying on this place. Whatever Elroy is up to, it looks like he can lead us to the Rippers."

"I can't stay here very long," Hawk said. "It's getting late. My mum will be expecting me on the Danforth about now."

"That's okay," Martin told him. "I'll watch the place until dark. I can come back tomorrow, too. I've got your cell number, Panny. I'll text you if anything happens, or if I need help. My aunt doesn't even notice if I stay out. And to be on the safe side, all I have to do is leave the TV on in my room. She'll fall asleep thinking I'm watching a game or something."

"Good idea, Martin. I'll walk part of the way home with our Hawk-boy here. Don't forget to call me if you need us — and stay out of the way of that Ripper gang!"

Martin settled down behind the Dumpster. Panny handed him a sandwich, a can of juice, and a candy bar. "Just don't fall asleep," she told him, shutting up her pannier again. "Okay, Hawk, let's walk!"

They waved goodbye to Martin, slipped away from Elroy's house, and headed north up Carlaw. They soon cut over to Logan, then walked north toward Gerrard.

"Cheer up, Hawk, Panny told him. "Sure, it seems impossible, but you'll get your glove back. Once the police break up that gang, all their loot will go back to the owners. And we might even help the cops crack down on those creeps."

"Yeah, I hope so," Hawk mumbled. "But I don't know if I can stand watching Elroy play with my glove and act as if he's owned it from day one."

"You don't want to worry about that right now. Save some of your energy for spying on this bunch, and for class. By the way, when are you coming in with us?"

"I don't know. It depends on my dad, I guess."

Panny wheeled along for a while without speaking, then suddenly turned to Hawk. "You're not scared of our class, are you?"

Hawk kicked at the sidewalk, grunted, then turned a fierce look on her, "Of course not! I've got good tests. I can do that work. The only reason I messed up was because Mrs. MacWhinney hated me."

"Oh yeah? And I guess you thought she was the cream of the crop? You did your best work for her?"

Hawk frowned and shook his head. "Well, it's true I didn't like her — but I did some good work for her too!"

"Don't worry! Ms. Calloway and Ms. Clarke are fair. They'll give you credit for your good work. And they'll help you. But don't mess around with them!"

For some reason what she was saying irritated Hawk. "Why would I mess around? Anyway, I don't even know if I want to go to your class. Everybody thinks they're great in there because they're all so gifted. I don't care about that, but they just better not make fun of me!"

Panny smiled at him. "Oh, that's what you're afraid of, is it? Well, I think you're tough enough to handle it. And I don't mean in a stupid way.... But look, I've got to take off. Chew-Boy needs a walk by now. You're okay on your own, aren't you?

"I'm not a baby, Panny. I know all these streets. I know all of Riverdale. And my dad took me around the city quite a few times. I might even know it better than you."

"Okay. I'll try to find you tomorrow after school. Then we can decide what to do about Elroy. I sure hope Martin is all right back there."

"Yeah, so do I."

Panny zoomed off, picking up speed as she wheeled away. Once she'd disappeared amid the traffic, Hawk began his jog, which soon turned into a sprint — he knew it was late, and he'd decided to go straight home. He didn't want any questions from his mum.

When he got to his own street, his breath was coming fast, and his chest hurt a little, but he pressed on, and after circling the Dumpsters, he caught sight of his mum pacing up and down beside the taxi, her scowl lingering even as he trotted up to her. "Where were you?" she demanded. "You were supposed to meet me on the Danforth!" At that moment he was very glad he'd made the extra effort.

"I'm not that late, Mum," he reassured her. "We played a bit longer than usual and I helped Mr. Rizzuto in the store."

"Don't you lie to me, Hawk. An Ojibway boy doesn't lie to his parents. I just talked to Mr. Rizzuto and he hasn't seen you since this morning."

Hawk stopped in his tracks, and thought very quickly. He smiled at his mother, moving closer and speaking in a placating "kid" voice that he seldom used. "Well, you see, Mum, I met this girl in the gifted class who wants to help me when I go in there. It'll make it much easier for me. She's really smart, and she knows all the kids. I was sure you'd want me to talk to her."

"Oh, yeah. Where'd you meet her?"

"Outside of Mr. Rizzuto's store." (Hawk was thinking how much easier it was to fib when your fibs were a version of the truth.)

His mother seemed to relax. She put her arm around him. "Okay, I hope she *can* help you. And I hope you listen. You hungry? Mr. Selim sent out some butter chicken."

"Wow! That's great. I'm starving."

A few minutes later they were sitting in the taxi, feasting on nan and the (slightly cold) butter chicken.

"There are a few things I want to talk over with you, Hawk. I don't want you to get upset about anything I say, but you've got to listen carefully, otherwise you might not do the right thing, and all my plans will be shot."

"Sure, Mum, I understand. Am I still going to see Dad tomorrow? Is he trying to get me into Panny's class? She's the girl who's been helping me. I think I can be okay in there, Mum, and I really wanna get back to school. She says they have good teachers there — not like Mrs. MacWhinney — and so many ways to help you learn things."

His mother didn't answer immediately, but gave him a sharp look. She paused and seemed to be considering something.

"All right, son. But I have to tell you — you know that you'll be going to see your father tomorrow. He wants to talk to you. He went over to speak with the board today after I did, to try to get you back into school, into the class you want."

"Great!"

"But there's something I have to remind you of. Just in case your father tries to spin things around. You're my son. I have custody, and you're bound to stay with me. Just remember that. Remember that your dad has no legal right to take you back, even though he has a right to see you. So you tell him so, you lay it on the line for him, if he tries to get you to stay with him!"

Hawk shook his head. Why was she going on about this? "You know I want to stay with you, Mum. You don't have to worry about it. I'll tell Dad I want to stay with you."

His mother smiled and looked relieved. She reached over, pulled him close, and gave him a hug. "Just remember you said that, son. I know you'll never regret it. We've been real happy together, haven't we?"

Hawk felt weighed down, but he managed a smile. "Sure, Mum."

Storm Cloud nodded and took a large sip from her container of coffee.

"I sure wish we could get a place with a stove," Hawk told her. "You have to drink coffee that's always cold. I eat cold food a lot of the time. We don't ever have hot water. I'm fed up living in this cab."

"I know — and that's exactly the second thing I wanted to talk about. I've got some news today. It may change the way we live. Son, would you believe it? I think we might be able to get out of this taxi and have a real apartment soon."

Hawk squirmed in his seat with excitement. "When? When?"

Storm Cloud smiled. "Oh, pretty soon. I heard from a friend in Ottawa today. She's a Native wife, just like me. The band up there is getting pretty active, doing protests and things, and they need volunteers. I mean, there's a bit of money in it, too, but the best thing is that if I go up there to help, they'll fix us up with an apartment. We won't have to live in this taxi anymore. And it could happen very, very soon."

Hawk felt a sinking in his stomach. His hands started shaking, and every fibre of his body moved to resistance. "Move to Ottawa? But Mum, I'm going to school here! I've got friends here. Mr. Rizzuto is helping me. I can make the Little League! We're kind of partners, too, Mr. Rizzuto and I are. We're looking for Babe Ruth's baseball. I might be a millionaire! I don't want to move to Ottawa. It's freezing, and there's nothing up there but politicians!"

His mother, disconcerted, swallowed the dregs of her coffee, squeezed the cup out of shape with her fingers, and gave him a very severe look. "Now, don't talk nonsense, Hawk! You'll go where your mother goes, and that's the end of it! I haven't quite decided on the move yet, but settling in Ottawa might be the best thing I could do for both of us. It's a dead end here, and we have to live in this stupid taxi and I have to sell crafts on the streets. If I can do something else in Ottawa, I'll love it there. You'll love it there, too. Don't go having a fit about nothing!"

"About *nothing*?" Hawk yelled.

"Now, that's enough! Let's not discuss it anymore. I just wanted to let you know what was happening — what might happen. Oh, wipe that sour look off your face — you look just like your dad when you make a face like that! We'll talk about this again when you're not so tired. Anyway, I brought you this comic I picked up on the Danforth. It should cheer you up. It looks like it's about a Native hero, too. Just enjoy it and don't worry about anything right now."

Hawk took a deep breath, reached out for the comic book, and slipped away into the front seat, hiding his swelling eyes from his mother. He didn't want to be a stupid crybaby, and he wouldn't! All the same, he felt miserable and had to fight off the tears until he got caught up in the story.

Didn't she know that everything was fine here and maybe getting better? Didn't she see that it wasn't worth moving to Ottawa even to get away from their miserable taxi?

He buried his head in the comic and tried to shut out the world. But even hours later, when darkness had settled down on the taxicab, the rough yard, and the blank buildings around, even as he fought to get to sleep, the terrible idea of moving away from his dad and his friends stuck with him. A blankness, a weight, seemed to hold him where he lay on the hard seat, and he squirmed restlessly to get comfortable.

Then, in the middle of his discomfort, something completely unexpected happened. There was a crash, a shattering of glass, a noise so close and so threatening that he jumped awake, shouting and swinging his arms in the darkness, as if to ward off the threat. He sat bolt upright. Something had showered on his clenched fists, something tangible and very real, like dust or small pebbles.

Seconds later his mother stood by the car. She yanked open his door, calling "Hawk! Hawk!" and pulling him out of the vehicle. She hugged him and he shook himself awake. Though he was shivering, he managed to reassure her.

"Mum, I'm okay. But look! Somebody threw a rock!"

His mother had managed to fetch her flashlight and together they examined the windshield, which had been shattered by something — an object, it seemed, hurled out of the darkness.

Sure enough, with the help of the flashlight they found a stone the size of a man's fist amid a shower of glass on the rough earth a few feet from the front of the car.

"This is terrible," his mother cried. "Who would do such a thing? Those damned street kids! If I ever catch them ..."

Hawk stood shivering. *Street kids?* His mother might have hit on something without knowing it. Hawk thought of the Ripper gang, of the sinister figure of Ringo with his tattoos, his ugly face, and his sneering manner.

He crossed his fingers then, and wished and hoped with all his heart that the gang hadn't caught Martin — that they hadn't figured out who was spying on them, and come in the night to take their revenge.

"If we had an apartment in Ottawa, or anywhere," his mother said, "something like this would never happen. Nothing will make me stay here after this!"

She kicked at the broken glass and seemed on the verge of tears. Hawk reached out and patted her hand.

Then there was nothing for them to do but crawl back into the shelter of the car and try to sleep.

Chapter 7

Father and Son

In the bright morning sunlight, Storm Cloud finished disposing of the broken windshield glass, and made sure that Hawk was properly washed and dressed to go and see his father.

"I'm not reporting this attack," she told her son. "It was probably just some stupid kids. If the police come to investigate, they'll probably kick us out of here, or at the very least send a report to the Children's Aid. You didn't mention it to Selim, did you?"

Hawk shook his head, then turned away, feeling guilty. After washing up and spending some time making faces at himself in the restroom mirror, he had run into Selim, the restaurant owner, and immediately told him about the stone-throwing. Noticing Selim's concern, he'd begged him not to let his mother know he'd told him.

"You're not going to call the police, are you, Mr. Selim?" he had asked.

Selim — a thin, neatly dressed man with large, dark eyes — shook his head, and said, "No, kid, but when you see your father, you tell him to get you out of here very soon. This is no place for a boy like you, or for your mother either. I won't tell anyone about last night, but if either of you get hurt, I'll be in big trouble."

Hawk felt things closing in. He knew his father would probably do nothing to help them, but still pinned his hopes on Mr. Rizzuto. Unlike his father, Mr. Rizzuto seemed very free and easy. His father seemed to be carrying some big burden, something that distracted him from dealing with Hawk or his mother directly. He didn't look forward to this morning's meeting, but he needed to get a promise from his father that he wouldn't be dragged up to Ottawa, even if it meant a better place to live. That and the school transfer were things his father might be able to help him with.

When Hawk was ready to leave, his mother said, "I won't go with you. I have to get over to my Danforth spot right away. We're running short of money again. You might drop a hint about that to your father. And remember what I told you about custody. You're staying with me — no matter what happens!"

Hawk gave his mother a parting hug, and began the trek up to the area where his father lived, a section of Riverdale called The Pocket. It was an area of solid old houses, quite expensive, but his father got the use of his house from the Native Centre, and paid no rent.

The closer he came to his dad's place, though, the more agitated Hawk felt. He remembered his dad — it seemed long ago — as a slim, strong man who spoke softly and wisely and seemed to know everything. Even then Hawk felt a little distant from him and was sometimes afraid of the man others called "Jim," or sometimes "Wolf." His father seemed very gloomy and moody at times, though when he laughed it was wonderful. Hawk found himself waiting for that laughter. Then, too, he had loved the baseball they played together, but as time passed his father seemed more and more distant and Hawk began to fear the moments when that calmness gave way, as it did once or twice, to fierce anger, rejection, or a sneering silence.

Hawk's mother was more predictable — always nervous, dissatisfied, quick and impulsive — and when she and his father started to disagree a few years before, Hawk had watched in despair as the two of them quarrelled, always louder, and without settling anything. As these quarrels continued, his father would disappear and stay away for days at a time. Then, one sad morning, Storm Cloud told Hawk that they were moving out. "Don't worry," she had told him, "you'll see your father quite often. It's all agreed."

Hawk had no idea what she was talking about and had burst into tears. After that, he stayed with his mother, and they moved from place to place, everything getting worse, until they finally had nowhere to stay but in the taxi. Hawk couldn't understand why his father didn't help them.

"He doesn't have much money," Storm Cloud had explained, "and he doesn't want me anywhere near him. He loves you, though, don't worry about that. If anything happens to me, he'll take care of you."

From time to time Hawk visited his father. They would eat hot dogs or hamburgers on the Danforth, go over to Riverdale Farm, or play baseball. "If you want to be a baseball player, you can make it," his father once told him. "Some Native people make it. Just look at Joba Chamberlain, one of the world champions."

Hawk was horrified when his glove was stolen, and was much too scared to tell his father about it. As he approached the old brick house on Condor Avenue, he wondered what he could say to his father — so many things had happened in the last few days. Life was scary, but exciting. He didn't want his father to shut down his adventures with Panny and Martin or his search with Mr. Rizzuto for Babe Ruth's lost baseball. And he didn't want his mother to haul him off to Ottawa either. When he climbed up the stairs and stood on the rickety porch of his father's house, he was trembling all over with excitement and trepidation.

He pressed the doorbell and almost immediately the door opened. His father came out, a big smile on his face. He grabbed Hawk, lifted him up, and gave him a fierce hug. "You made it okay — that's good!"

he said, setting his son down and gazing at him with his penetrating dark eyes.

"Good to see you, kid. You look okay, terrific, in fact, although maybe a little tired." His father hesitated for a moment, glancing up and down the empty street. "Your mother didn't bring you over?"

Hawk stepped confidently into the house. "Nah, I walked over myself."

His father followed him in, shutting the door gently behind him. "I don't like you walking all over the city. It's not that safe for kids your age."

"Don't worry, Dad, I have friends, And Mum keeps track of where I am."

"All right. Well, you're here. I guess you're hungry, so let's eat before we talk."

His father led the way into the kitchen. It was at the back of the house, a little dark and in need of a paint job, but neat and tidy. Hawk enjoyed sitting in that kitchen. To him it seemed enormous, yet cozy, and he always felt happy there.

His father hauled out some plates and heated up a few hamburgers and chips in the microwave. They sat at the table, and when the food came, Hawk helped himself to the mustard and ketchup. He drank the orange soda his father poured, but after a few gulps he couldn't wait any longer to get to what was bothering him.

"Dad, Mum's thinking of moving to Ottawa. I don't want to go there."

His father looked at him across the table, but went right on eating. Hawk started getting nervous

— his father's silent moods always scared him. In his khaki shirt and jeans, his dad looked like a cool cowboy from some western movie; but of course he wasn't a cowboy, he was an "Indian." He was on the other team, one of the bad guys, the dangerous ones. That's how the white folks told it, long ago. But now it was different. He saw the familiar poster on the grey-white wall behind his father: JIM EAGLESON SPEAKS ON NATIVE RIGHTS. His father, a proud Native, told the real story — a better story.

If only he would say something now.

But his father went on, methodically finishing his lunch. "Another burger?" he asked at last, but Hawk was impatient. "Maybe before I go."

Jim smiled. "Eager to have a talk, are you? All right then, let's go sit in the living room."

Hawk nodded and stepped into the next room. He settled himself on the old sofa underneath the window and swallowed the last of his drink. While his father cleaned up a bit in the kitchen, Hawk got up and wandered around the room, taking in the familiar objects and pictures. There was an old tribal drum and some headdresses and shawls, his grandfather's Colt revolver and riding gear, photographs of his father in tribal dress and, half-naked, coming out of a sweat lodge. There were plants and a small aquarium, a jar with a pipe and some tobacco, and on the wall a couple of Chevy hubcaps that a clever artist had turned into crazy sculptures.

"There's good news about the school," his father said, coming through the doorway. "You can go over there tomorrow. Your mother made a good case for you. You're lucky she's so relentless … but what's this about moving to Ottawa?"

"She thinks we can get an apartment there. Somebody promised her a job, sort of a job, and a place to live. Dad, almost anything would be better than that taxi, but I don't want to move to Ottawa!"

Hawk felt his voice cracking, and swallowed hard. He didn't want to break down in front of his father.

Jim sat down, bent his head, and pressed the palm of his right hand to his forehead — a familiar, weary gesture. Without looking at Hawk, he said in a low, flat voice, "No, no … you won't go to Ottawa, even if your mum moves up there. And it might be a good thing for her, unless she's dreaming again. But if she does go, you can come here. Anyway, we've got to get you out of that taxi. That's not a good neighbourhood you're in either, what with those gangs and tough guys. I'm sorry I've had to leave you there, but your mum isn't easy to deal with."

Hawk hardly knew what to say. Now his father had mentioned gangs and street kids … but he just couldn't tell him about the lost glove. He couldn't say anything about yesterday's tracking of Elroy either, even though he was proud of what he, Panny, and Martin were doing to get his glove back. But if he mentioned their spying activities, his father would crack down. He was already worried about him walking around alone in Riverdale. He sure wouldn't like him trying to outsmart street gangs and thugs!

Hawk sat there confused. He started to speak and then cut himself off. Jim watched him with his strong, focused glance, and Hawk thought he could see a flicker of amusement in his dad's eyes.

"Listen, son," his father said, "I don't think you know it, but your mother's already told me about the glove and the way those kids pushed you around. Damned bullies, that's what they are! I didn't want to mention it until you did, but probably this is a good time. I know you're upset about it, but don't worry, I'm going to get you another glove. But first I want to see you in school, a *good* school, with *good* teachers. And out of that taxi as soon as possible. But everything's a little tricky. If I try to do too much, your mum will scream. She wants the best for you, but she's a difficult woman. I bet right now she's up on the Danforth, selling her 'Native artifacts.' It's nothing but a joke. It works against everything I'm trying to achieve. I wish I could —"

"She's almost out of money, too, Dad," Hawk interrupted. "That's why she sells that stuff. Of course she likes to make things, too. She'd never ask you for money, but maybe you could help her a little."

His father bristled. "Damn it, son, now she's got you begging money for her! Why can't she just ask me if she needs something?"

Hawk gulped and stiffened. He couldn't bear his father's anger, and sat there, hardly daring to breathe or move, silently praying that his dad wouldn't explode.

But Jim didn't blow up; he merely growled, muttered, and shook his head, then gradually seemed to settle down. He looked up sheepishly at Hawk. "So, how's the baseball going?" he asked. "Mr. Rizzuto teaching you some good tricks? You're going to make the Little League team this time, right?"

"Sure, Dad. You bet I will!" Hawk basked in his father's half-smile, and was relieved that he was trying to keep things cool. That made him happier, but a small amount of guilt lingered. He badly wanted to tell his dad about Mr. Rizzuto's plan to search for Babe Ruth's baseball, how exciting it was, and how it might make them all rich, but he just couldn't bring it up. His father would see it all as crazy stuff, and would turn against it. "Let's keep things down-to-earth," his dad used to say, whenever Hawk did a mental spacewalk. "No pipe dreams." And Storm Cloud would contradict him: "Leave the boy alone! There's no hope at all without dreams, even pipe dreams, and that's a fact a Cree warrior ought to recognize."

Hawk remembered this, but was anxious to steer the conversation to more comfortable subjects, and wasn't sure he was succeeding. "Could I see Grandpa's Colt again, and could we play catch in the backyard for a while?"

His father nodded. "Okay, why not? Now that we've had our talk … and you seem to understand where we're at, let's do that."

Jim crossed the room, reached down, and pulled a baseball bat, a glove, and a ball out from behind the couch. As he blew the dust off the objects, he made a face. "Guess it's been too long since we had these out," he said.

"How about Grandpa's gun?" Hawk asked. "Can I look at it?

"Can I look at it first?" His father smiled, hesitated, put down the bat, ball, and glove, and lifted the glass top of the display case that sat on the table under the sculptures.

He picked up the gun, checked it over, and handed it to his son. It was an impressive thing, with its carved wooden handle and long metal barrel. To Hawk it seemed very heavy, and also powerful, almost a magic object, very different from the guns he saw occasionally in his comic books. He cradled it in his hands, which suddenly looked smaller, then pretended to fire it, choosing an imaginary enemy hiding somewhere behind the bushes in the driveway.

"I wish I'd had this the night the Rippers stole my glove," he said.

His father shook his head and looked serious. "Not a good thought," he warned. "Grandfather Eagleson wouldn't have liked to hear that — although I know you're just speculating. He was peaceful man, though when he worked in the rodeos they sometimes got him into shooting contests on the side. He was a good shot and very proud of his gun, which he won in a contest, proud of it because it's a thing of beauty and worth keeping. A Colt Peacemaker — Buntline Special — a well-made weapon. Your grandfather knew that, but he also remembered much about how guns just like it had been used against innocent people, and against our people. When he gave it to me he made me swear I'd never load any bullets in it, except for very special demonstrations. I've only done it once in my life, and that was to impress your mother. Otherwise, I treat it as something to look at and touch, not to use."

"If somebody broke into this house, would you kill them with it?" Hawk asked suddenly.

"No way. I'd try to discourage them by other means, but I'd never shoot them."

"Suppose they were going to kill Mum or me? Would you use it then?"

Jim grunted, and looked a bit askance. He shrugged his shoulders and replied, "You do ask questions, don't you? No … the answer is *no*. I'd find another way."

"Will you leave this to me when you die, Dad?"

"Sure, but on the same terms your grandfather set.… Hey, now, enough of that stuff! Let's put the gun back and try some baseball. I want to see what you've learned from that Rizzuto fellow."

Hawk frowned, nodded, then shoved the gun awkwardly into his belt, only to draw it out again very quickly, as if challenged by some invisible enemy.

"Got him!" he said, pretending to fire the thing again — one last shot with the magic weapon.

"Time for baseball," his father insisted, gently slipping the gun from Hawk's grasp. He looked at it, rubbed it on his jeans as if he were polishing it, then carefully put it back in the display case.

Hawk looked on, frowning, feeling sorry that his moment of power was over. Then he shrugged, gathered up bat, ball, and glove, and followed his father through the kitchen and into the backyard.

Hawk and his father set up a net and whacked at the tennis ball for an hour or so. A couple of times when the batted ball went astray, the ancient and very grumpy lady who lived in the house behind the back fence appeared. She had glowered a few times at Hawk during his past visits, and again today she came out and gave them a look, but Jim just waved at her and smiled.

"She doesn't like our fun," his father growled, "but she won't dare say anything. Probably thinks I'll put on war paint and shoot burning arrows at her porch if she does!"

When it was time for Hawk to go, his father disappeared for a moment, returning with a small brown envelope, which he shoved into Hawk's jacket pocket.

"Give this to your mother," he said. "Too bad it's not enough to get her off the Danforth.... But don't talk to her about that Ottawa deal of hers — just leave it to me. You won't be going up there if I can help it. And I *can* help it!"

Chapter 8

On the Danforth

Hawk waved goodbye to his dad and headed for the Danforth. His visits with his dad were great, but somehow he always felt sad when he left. It wasn't just because he was leaving either. He'd finally figured out that it was because he knew he'd never have a regular home with his mum and dad again. He was always going to be a visitor with one or the other.

Hawk sighed, frowned, and squeezed his father's envelope tightly in his pocket. Jim hadn't said so, but he knew he shouldn't look at it. Luckily, his mother wasn't far away, so he wouldn't be tempted.

Storm Cloud had moved east on the Danforth, past Jones Avenue. She'd explained to Hawk that she and a couple of friends had chosen a corner located close to a Buddhist temple, and not far from a liquor store. "If they follow their religion, we ought to do okay," she told him. "Otherwise we can profit from those folk who like to drink but feel awful guilty about it."

Although Hawk's mother had gone begging a few times, she had sworn never to do it again. As she had explained to Hawk, it was a terrible life: stony-faced business types just ignoring you, or bigots who would glare at you then tell you to "go back to the reservation." Hawk shuddered when he thought of it. Now his mother and her friends were into selling, not begging. They had worked out a deal with a "nearly new" shop owner to set up on the sidewalk outside her store. That made it look like a sidewalk sale and kept the other store-owners happy — and the police out of the picture.

Storm Cloud had amassed several boxes of crafts — tiny dolls, drums, animal figures, and leather footwear and bags — all of which Selim allowed her to keep in a spare room and which she drew on when she set up her table. Today it was animal figures and drums, sandals and change purses, while her East Indian friends displayed small bottles, placemats with pictures of tigers on them, and carrying bags stamped with the Taj Mahal. Unfortunately, they had all gotten off to a late start and missed most of the lunch crowd.

Hawk waved to his mother and sheepishly greeted the other ladies — a small brown-skinned woman with dark eyes and rough, pockmarked skin, and a tall woman dressed in jeans and a yellow blouse. They were setting up their tables and furtively casting glances at the people streaming past — potential customers, most of them indifferent.

"Where've you been?" Storm Cloud asked, pouncing on Hawk before he could catch his breath. "Don't tell me you spent all this time with your dad?"

Hawk started to tell her about his visit, but his mother interrupted. "What did he say about us moving to Ottawa?"

"He didn't say much," Hawk fibbed. "He said he'd talk to you about it. He doesn't like us to live in the taxi anymore. And by the way, he gave me this."

Hawk thrust the brown envelope at Storm Cloud, who grabbed it and glanced around at her friends, looking embarrassed. She shoved it into her pocket without a word.

"What are we going to do about the taxi, Mum?" Hawk asked. "We can't go back to that wreck. And somebody must be after us."

Hawk was still wondering if the Rippers had tracked him home. If they knew that he and his friends were spying on them, had they smashed the window of the car to scare him off? He couldn't tell his mother a thing, but needed to talk to Panny or Martin about it. What would happen if it was the gang? Would they come back that night?

"We'll figure out something," his mother said, trying to reassure him, even though she only knew half the story. "I'm betting it was just some stupid kid throwing stones. Don't worry about it right now — you should be thinking of school."

"Yeah, I am thinking about it," Hawk said. He was trying his best to sound enthusiastic, although he felt a little anxious about what was coming. *Would the kids make fun of him? Would they decide that he was ignorant or stupid?* He swallowed his fears, and to placate his mother, he added, "Dad says you did a good job dealing with the School Board."

"Oh, he did, did he? Well, he's right about that. I got you in there. Not many people in my position could have managed it. The rest is up to you."

"Don't worry, Mum, I won't disappoint you."

"I know you won't. Now just sit in that chair over there while we finish setting up these tables."

Hawk spent the next forty-five minutes watching his mother and her friends trying to sell their wares to the passersby. A steady stream of people marched past, hardly any of them taking notice of the three women who stood by the tables attempting to catch their attention, discreetly announcing "nice bags," "bottles," "Native crafts," and other things that drew hardly a look, but caused quite a few pedestrians to step ahead all the faster when they heard them.

Among them were young, well-dressed women hurrying back from late lunches, housewives pushing strollers, delivery men in grey uniforms, a few old codgers stealing a smoke, teens texting and joking with one another as they marched past, and one policeman, who gave the sellers a quick glance before moving on. No one stopped except a couple of very old ladies wrapped in shabby shawls, who for a few minutes poked among the dolls and the placemats, the bottles and the toy drums, then shook their heads disapprovingly and trudged away.

It was depressing, Hawk thought, like a garage sale on a dead-end street — why did his mother have to do this? This was the Danforth, where everyone seemed busy buying and selling, a street with coffee shops, restaurants, small stores, and endless traffic, a place where no one wanted what these ladies had to sell. After an hour they hadn't got rid of a single item and Hawk was desperate to escape.

He sat squirming in his seat, thinking about what it would be like to be rich — to live in a nice house, to own a store, to drive a car, to walk right past people selling stupid things. Not to feel scared or guilty about anything.

Then, in the middle of his sad, confused thoughts, a bell tinkled cheerily, a familiar figure zoomed up the sidewalk on her bike, braked to a stop a few feet from where he sat, and greeted him. "Hey, Hawk-boy, what's this street stuff? I've a got a few things to tell you."

"Panny! How did you know I was here?"

The girl smiled, slipped from her bike, and, with a glance at the three women, quietly told him, "One of my friends spotted you and texted me. I've got news from Martin. He followed Elroy to a place that might be important — a warehouse south of Lakeshore. We need to know more about that, and I think we've got a plan."

"Great!" Hawk jumped up and down with excitement. Storm Cloud eyed them and started over.

He whispered quickly to Panny, "Here's my mum. Don't mention this. We're talking about school, understand? She got me in. I start tomorrow."

"Don't worry about the teachers," Panny told him, speaking in a loud, clear voice. "You'll like the class, too. Everything will be fine."

She turned to greet Hawk's mother. "Hello, I'm Panny. You must be Hawk's mother. I'm in his new class. He's transferring tomorrow, right?"

"That's right," Storm Cloud told her, sizing up the confident Panny. "I hope you can help Hawk fit in. I hope your class is friendly. He's a smart boy, you know, which his teachers don't seem to understand."

"Oh, don't worry about that," Panny reassured her. "We have two great teachers. And the class is fine. I was just going to fill in your Hawk on that. Give him a few tips. Maybe we could go for a Coke while you're busy here."

Storm Cloud looked a little doubtful, but then with a glance at her selling table, still ignored by every passerby, she nodded. "Well, I guess so, but only for fifteen or twenty minutes. I'm just about to wrap up here. It hasn't been a very good day."

Hawk knew she had the envelope with his dad's money in her pocket, and that the day hadn't been a total waste. "We'll be back really soon, Mum," he promised.

The kids moved off quickly. Panny wheeled her bike along the sidewalk. "There's a bench down the street," she said. "We can talk for a few minutes."

"Somebody threw a rock at our taxi," Hawk told her. "Do you think one of the gang followed Martin? Did he go looking for me? I can't figure it out."

Panny looked grim. "That's scary," she said. "The sooner we get the police into this, the better. But Martin wasn't followed — he told me he was very careful. I bet what happened was that Elroy told the gang that you were suspicious of him, and they decided to scare you. Since they'd stolen your glove in your neighbourhood, it would be no trick to figure out where you hung out. How many old taxis have a kid and his mum living in them?"

"Gee, that's right. I think that must be what happened."

"Sure it is! But listen, Hawk, Martin and I have a new idea. See what you think. Next baseball practice you and Martin have to go after Elroy and get him real scared. We think he might head off to check things out with the gang. Remember, we don't think he's one of them — they're probably just testing him out. Probation, right? Martin can track him and learn some more about where the gang hangs out and who's in it. Then maybe we can tell the police."

"Great! Sounds okay to me," Hawk told her. He wasn't so sure that things would run so smoothly, but what else could they do?

"Good," Panny said. "But I've got to go now. I cut out of a few important duties to come here. I'll see you tomorrow, anyway."

"Yeah, I'd better go back," Hawk said. "My mum looked a little suspicious. You know things are tricky between her and my dad. Now she wants to take me to Ottawa."

"Ottawa! Oh my God!"

"Don't worry. My dad won't let it happen. He promised me, although she doesn't know it."

"Wow, Hawk-boy. You have a complicated life. But don't worry — I think things will get better for you."

"Yeah, I hope so. See you tomorrow, Panny."

Panny swung her bike around, waved, and zoomed back along the Danforth. Hawk went and bought a Coke, sat on the bench for a while, then walked slowly back to his mother. Pedestrians, still not buying anything, tramped past the table, but their numbers had thinned out. The afternoon was waning. The other two women had already departed and Storm Cloud was packing up.

"I guess we'd better go home now," his mother said. "Nobody's buying anything today. I just saw that Panny shoot past. She flies around on her bike like some kind of elf-girl, doesn't she? I sure hope she gave you some good advice about tomorrow."

Chapter 9

School Bells and Surprises

Hawk trudged home with his mother, helping her carry some of the unsold items from her table. They said very little to each other on the way, but after a while Storm Cloud asked him, "Where does this Panny live?"

"In Chinatown, near Mr. Rizzuto's store. She has a dog named Chew-Boy. I saw her once in the schoolyard."

"She seems smart enough.... A nice friend.... Maybe we should get a watchdog for our hangout?"

"I don't think it would do much good," Hawk said. "It would be some old stray that would just run away."

They walked on in silence until they finally reached their street. Right away, both noticed that something had changed.

"Somebody moved one of the Dumpsters!" Hawk shouted as he started to run forward.

"Be careful!" his mother warned. She scrambled along, trying to keep up.

When they reached their familiar maze of lots and back alleys, they both stopped in their tracks.

"Somebody's taken our taxi!" Storm Cloud cried out.

Hawk stared around at the nearly empty yard: a few beat-up barrels and oil cans, a pile of tires, a litter of broken window frames, and a stack of rotting lumber — but no taxi — and no place to sleep for the night.

Hawk sprang forward, studying the muddy patch and the big ruts where the taxi had been, and then examining the cast-off wrappers and half-crushed plastic cups that lay strewn about the yard.

"Mum! Some big machinery's been in here. Some kind of tow truck. And the guys were eating snacks and drinking coffee. They must have moved the Dumpster and then hauled the car away. Who did this? What are we going to do? Where are we going to stay?"

His mother looked around, but didn't say anything for a long time. Finally, she shook her head sadly and said, "I don't know, Hawk. I hated that taxi, but I could kill them for this! Someone must have complained to the city."

Hawk stood shivering. *Was it the gang? Did they have friends at City Hall?* He knew from his comic books, and what he'd heard, that gangsters sometimes had such connections. Even the Rippers might be able to hurt them in that way. Everything seemed to be against them. He wished his father was there; he would know what to do.

They were still standing there, undecided and feeling quite helpless, when the back door of the restaurant opened and Selim emerged. Thin, neatly dressed in white, and smiling, he moved with his quick catlike poise in their direction.

"So you're back!" he said. He nodded to Storm Cloud and patted Hawk gently on the shoulder. "You look puzzled — the famous taxi has vanished! I'm glad you missed our little show. That was my plan. I didn't want you to be upset or to feel altogether displaced. Home is home, after all. But I really had to do something about that taxi."

"*You* got rid of it, Mr. Selim?" Hawk asked, relieved now, and excited.

But, though the little man nodded and looked pleased, Storm Cloud glared at him. "Just great! I had some stuff stashed in that car. And where are we going to sleep tonight?"

"Have no fear, Mrs. Ruby," (which was what Selim always chose to call her) "I will give you a room at the back of the restaurant. I put your stuff in there already. It's only temporary, but much better than the wrecked automobile. I can give you one month there, free, plenty of time to find something else."

When Storm Cloud's stormy look failed to lift, he added, "It's dangerous, you know. What with people throwing stones at the car. If I didn't do something, I would certainly get in trouble with the police and the inspectors. And your boy here, brave as he is, might get hurt. Don't worry, you'll be better off in the little room I have for you. But just remember, it is for one month only. Please make other arrangements as soon as you can. It's for your own good."

Hawk listened to all this, then, seeing that his mother wasn't convinced, piped up. "Hey, Mum, it's much better to be inside with me starting school and all. I can get some sleep and I have a place to study. It's a great idea, don't you think?"

His mother sighed and nodded as she looked around helplessly. "Okay, Mr. Selim. Can we see the room?"

Selim led the way. Inside the long rear entrance corridor of the restaurant, between the washroom and the back door, he pointed to another room. Hawk had passed the door often, but it was always locked, and he'd assumed it was a storeroom. One look inside told him it was, or had been, just that: grey walls, peeling paint, a dim ceiling light, a narrow slot of a window, barred and cobwebbed, and boxes piled high in one corner. But also two cots, a card table holding a hotplate and an ornamental lamp, and even a small fridge, plugged into the wall and humming away.

"You see, all the comforts of home," Selim told them. "There's some food in the fridge, too. Enjoy the shelter. But remember, please, only for one month."

Storm Cloud gazed around. Hawk was surprised. She seemed on the verge of tears. He couldn't figure out why. This was much better than their taxi.

Selim nodded as if pleased with his own arrangements, but when Storm Cloud said nothing, he patted Hawk on the shoulder and quietly slipped away.

"It's not so bad, Mum," Hawk told her. "I like it here. It's a good place to study. And nobody can throw rocks at us. We're safe here, Mum. And don't worry. We've got a whole month to find something. Maybe I'll have that Babe Ruth baseball by then, and we can move into a hotel. Dad can find us one, I'll bet."

His mother cleared her throat and made a disparaging sound with her lips. "Your father? He's useless, that man! Just look at where we've ended up. I wouldn't ask *him* for any favours. I can't wait to get out of this city and get an apartment of my own! You'll see, Hawk, we can do much better than this!"

Hawk was puzzled at her bitterness, but within a few hours they had settled down, eaten some of the tandoori chicken and cold rice that Selim had left for them in the fridge, and generally made themselves at home. Storm Cloud rummaged in a bag that Selim had rescued from the trunk of the taxi and laid out some clothes for Hawk.

"School tomorrow!" she reminded him, just before they turned out the light. "I'll get you up when it's time."

Hawk had a restless sleep and woke up first. It was a bit late, he noticed, as he shook his mother awake. They cleaned up in the restaurant washroom, ate a few bites of the leftovers, and hurried off toward the school.

It was not a long walk, but all the way there Hawk was thinking, *I'm going back to school!* He kept catching his breath and couldn't decide whether he was a bit scared or just very excited.

Rawson School, an old red-brick school not far from Chinatown, was familiar enough. It had been the scene of his earlier conflicts with the terrible Mrs. MacWhinney. Despite their best efforts, Hawk and his mum were a little bit late, and Storm Cloud led the way, first into the main office and from there, with the blessings of the principal, to his new classroom.

It was all so easy, except that, at the head of the stairs, he glanced into a classroom through an open door and caught a glimpse of an animated, irritated Mrs. MacWhinney chastising some poor student.

Hawk made a nasty hand gesture at the frozen-faced woman and hurried on with his mother.

"Uh, uh, uh," said a blonde woman standing in the doorway of the next classroom. "None of that, young man!" Storm Cloud, who had also seen his reaction, gave him a withering look. "Nice way to begin," she murmured.

"This must be Hawk," said the teacher. "Hello, Hawk. Hello, Mrs. Wilson — I'm Ms. Calloway. Ms. Clarke and I are the teachers for Grade Four Gifted. Ms. Clark will be here tomorrow. We're glad you could join our class. I've asked Panny Chang to show you your seat."

Hawk slipped into the class. A smiling Panny greeted him and pointed to a seat in the middle of the classroom. "Good luck, Hawk-boy," she whispered.

The classroom was bright and airy. The seats were lined up in twos, facing each other, and ran up the middle of the large room. The blackboard at the front was almost invisible, covered with lists and charts. There were posters on the windows reading ARTS ALIVE, SCIENCE ROCKS, and LITERATURE FOR LIFE. A huge sign hung above the rear blackboard advising EXPLORE YOUR MULTIPLE INTELLIGENCES. Beside it were pinned large photos of famous people illustrating the various human gifts, skills, or "intelligences" — verbal, logical, mathematical, musical, interpersonal, and several others.

Hawk recognized Einstein, Mahatma Gandhi, Hayley Wickenheiser, and Mother Teresa among them. A number of computers were lined up on a long table, and there was a washstand and a display table piled high with class projects — imposing models of castles, jousts, and tournaments, a paper maché cathedral, and other 3-D representations of what looked like scenes from the Middle Ages. Finally, Hawk spotted a wall of books, neatly sorted and stashed in plastic milk cases.

He swallowed hard and flopped down at his desk, staring at the maps and charts, and at the personal laptop computers on several students' desks. He listened in amazement to the low hum of chatter that filled the room. The kids were working on some kind of project, and most of them were focused on that, although a few were stealing a look at their favourite books of the moment, while one or two seemed to be just fooling around.

When Ms. Calloway returned to her desk a few moments later, she zeroed in on the chatterers and got them to quiet down. Then she darted around the room, advising here and there, lifting books from the distracted and getting them back on course, and finally stopping beside Hawk's desk.

"Can I talk to you for a minute, Hawk, at my desk?"

Hawk jumped up and followed her. He felt the eyes of several of the kids on him, and heard whispers behind his back.

"Get back to your work!" Ms. Calloway ordered. She sat down and motioned the boy to a folding chair beside her desk.

"Now, Hawk, I know you started the year in another class. You realize that the board has made a very big exception in transferring you at this date?"

He nodded, somewhat overawed by her strong presence. She didn't look like a teacher, more like a woman on TV, someone who might speak out for some good cause: the homeless, refugees, or the environment maybe. She wore a white blouse and jeans, and had curly blonde hair and metal earrings that swung as she spoke. She had a nice smile and clear blue eyes, but he didn't think she'd put up with any nonsense.

Ms. Calloway continued. "If you do well in our class, you might be promoted to Gifted Grade Five, but that will require that you *really* do well. We'll be helping you. We want you to succeed. You've got the ability — your tests show that — but you haven't done that well so far. I realize it won't be easy, since you haven't been with us the whole year, but we'll try to catch you up. Ms. Clarke and I agree on this. Come to either of us if you need help, understand?"

Hawk nodded. "Sure, Ms. ... Thanks!"

"All right then. Pay attention to what's happening in here, and when your turn comes, do your best. Everybody's unique, and you've got a lot to contribute, I'm sure."

Then, to his acute embarrassment, Ms. Calloway introduced him to the class. "This is Hawk Wilson, who has come to us late in the year. All the more reason we should encourage him and help him to become a real contributor to this class! Let's welcome him, Room 21, all together now!"

There was applause and a few cheers. Blushing, Hawk returned to his seat. He refused to look around, but took out his pencils and the pad his mother had bought him. Then he noticed a small piece of paper on his desk, folded like the message in a fortune cookie. He opened it up and read, *Hi, Pocahontas. What kind of hairspray do you use?*

Chapter 10

Dangerous Connections

Hawk felt as if he'd been slapped in the face. He crumpled up the paper and threw it on the floor.

Someone hissed a warning. He looked up and saw Panny giving him a "what's going on?" look. He shrugged his shoulders and opened his notebook.

"Now we're going to have three personal contributions on the Middle Ages from those of you who wrote your essays on medieval themes," Ms. Calloway announced. "Rahul, do you want to go first?"

"Okay."

A short, stocky boy got out of his seat and headed for the front of the class. He was wearing dark trousers and a bright white shirt that contrasted nicely with his glossy black hair and cinnamon-coloured skin.

"I wrote my essay on the monasteries," he reminded them. "My personal creative contribution is a story I've written about a monk who finds a manuscript from Roman times, one that tells about the Greek gods, which, when he reads it, makes him lose his faith in Christ and start believing in Zeus, Hermes, Artemis, and the other gods. But first I'll remind you of their Roman names."

Hawk sat wide-eyed, wondering if this boy was some kind of genius, or maybe he had swallowed a USB memory stick that some history professor had lost.

The talk went on for a while. Hawk sat transfixed. Afterward there were several questions, and even a correction or two.

"I think you've got a couple of the attributes of Hermes wrong," a girl in sparkly jeans suggested.

Ms. Calloway led a brief discussion about the transition from the pagan gods to Christianity. There were a few probing questions. Hawk looked on, amazed. He was trying desperately to remember the rough dates for the Middle Ages.

The second "personal contribution" was a modern rewriting of Chaucer's "The Pardoner's Tale." Hawk had a vague notion that Chaucer was some kind of famous poet of the Middle Ages, but he didn't even know what a pardoner was. The presenter this time was a boy named Albert Mostley, a chubby, bespectacled kid with unruly red hair. His vocabulary was enormous and he dropped in a few side remarks that had the class roaring with laughter.

By the time this presentation was over, Hawk had learned a lot about Chaucer — and his world — but he was also ready to run out of the room and disappear. What kind of class had he landed in? He would never make it with this bunch. "Smarts" were one thing, but being a walking, breathing, ad-libbing encyclopedia was another!

The last talk, however, really sank his hopes. A student named Wang got up, a nearsighted, slender boy with a crewcut and a "Walk for Cancer" T-shirt, and proceeded to trace out the relations between medieval Europe and China. Not only did he flash maps of the trade routes, and charts of important dates and personages, but he offered them a comparison between the main dialects of Chinese and those of Turkish middlemen on the Spice Road between east and west using, of course, the original languages and explaining the most important Chinese characters and how they had changed over the centuries.

This talk was so knockout smart that Hawk didn't expect any tough class questions, but there were a couple, and Ms. Calloway mentioned a few things about the spice road that even young Wang didn't know. She also promised to play the class some music by a Canadian singer who had travelled that route a few years before and had written music about her experiences with different cultures.

Minutes later came the lunch break. Of course, Hawk hadn't brought any lunch, and he wandered out of the room in a daze, wondering if he should head home then, or just wait to get kicked out of the class when his turn came to show his work.

He was looking around for Panny, who seemed to have been delayed in the classroom, when a tall, dark-haired boy approached him and shook his hand, "My name is Charles," he said. "Welcome to the class." Hawk mumbled a thanks. The boy had a bright and glittering smile that Hawk didn't quite like.

"You got my note?" the boy asked. "Just a little joke, of course. It doesn't matter if you're Native. I'm inviting you into my club anyway. It's a special group — called the Ferrets. The members are all my friends. It's a secret society and the teachers don't know, so if you say a word to anyone, you're toast. I mean *anyone*. It would be a good idea to join. There's an initiation, of course — and there's dues. I have lots of members, though, and I can protect you, because you'll work for me."

With that the tall boy drifted off to join a couple of his friends who had stood by smirking as they watched the proceedings with a fixed, goggle-eyed intensity.

Hawk just stood there, stunned. Slowly, he wandered down the hall, past the gabbing, joking kids. No one paid him much attention. He wondered what he had gotten into, coming to this school. These kids were all too weird. Too smart in the wrong way. Scary. Maybe he *should* head home right away. He felt so confused; he didn't know what to do.

"Hello! Hawk! Wait a minute, please." Ms. Calloway stood at the classroom door, calling after him. She beckoned to him and he drifted slowly back.

"You were going to the lunchroom, I suppose," she said. "We don't sell food at the school, Hawk, and it looks like you haven't brought any." Ms. Calloway smiled, but her voice was warm and somehow reassuring.

"Panny had to stay behind a minute to talk to me about her presentation, but she and Albert are going to share with you," she told him. "In fact, here they are now. I hope you're going to enjoy your time with us, Hawk. I'll want you to do a presentation to the class, but in your case I think we can expand the subject a bit. So give some thought to what you want to talk about."

"Okay.... Thanks, Ms. Calloway."

Panny and Albert slid up beside him and Albert tapped him on the shoulder. "You can have half my ham sandwich," he said. "I wouldn't do that for just anyone," he added.

"And I've got an extra muffin," Panny said. "Bring some food tomorrow, Hawk-boy!"

Ms. Calloway laughed and turned back to her classroom.

"So, what was bugging you in there?" Panny asked. "You made a face and threw something on the floor like it was a bad message from a fortune cookie."

Hawk thought at once of Charles's warning: *If you say a word to anyone, you're toast.* He couldn't just blab. He had to learn more about the Ferrets. Maybe this was a test. *Maybe Panny and Albert were part of it!*

"So?" Panny waited for his answer.

"Oh, nothing," Hawk lied. I was just ticked off that I'd forgotten my lunch. I was pretty sure I couldn't buy anything here and I was getting hungry."

"You want that sandwich right now?" Albert asked.

"No, that's okay. I feel better now.... Except that I don't think I belong in this class. Those presentations were over the top. It would take me five years to do something like that."

"Oh? It only took me a few hours," Albert said. "Actually, I wrote a whole detective story based on 'The Pardoner's Tale' and was going to recite it in Middle English, but I thought it would just confuse the class."

"Stop bragging," Panny told him. "You know what Ms. Calloway says. We have to celebrate other people's achievements, not just brag about our own. Now we have a chance to help the Hawk-boy get over his worries about being able to do a presentation."

"I don't have any worries," Hawk said.

"Okay, you don't have any worries, but we can still help you," Panny insisted. "Now let's eat!"

They came to the bottom of the stairs and entered the lunchroom, a large space already packed with dozens of kids from various parts of the school. Hawk gazed around, dazzled by the noise, the buzzing energy, the ordered chaos of the place. Almost at once, he spotted Charles, ensconced with some of their classmates in a nearby corner. The dark-haired boy nodded vaguely at him and made a face. Hawk couldn't quite read his expression, but he knew he didn't like it.

The three friends settled down together at the end of a long table and began their meal. With a resigned look, Albert passed half his sandwich over to Hawk. After the first few bites of food and a couple of sips of their shared juices, Panny said, "Okay, Hawk. So you have to do a presentation. Well, I have an idea for you — take it or leave it."

"What is it?" Hawk mumbled, reaching for one of the juice cans.

"You should give a talk on Native life and customs or history," Panny suggested. "We hear a lot about Greece, Rome, the Middle Ages, the Jews, the Arabs, the Chinese — but almost nothing about our Native Canadian people. Does that interest you at all?"

Hawk thought about it. He might be able to do it, but would his father despise him for it, thinking that his mother had suggested it? Would his mother try to take it over? And would he be able to dig up enough material — material that the kids would be interested in and take seriously? All of this weighed on him. He knew it would take up a lot of time; time he'd hoped to spend with Mr. Rizzuto looking for Babe Ruth's lost baseball. He hadn't dared speak of that quest to his father, and he was still a bit shy to tell his new friends about it — they might laugh at him and tell him to "get real."

"I don't know," he said to Panny. "I don't know if I should do that."

"Why not? Isn't your father active in Native rights? I'm sure he'd be able to help you. You can call him on my phone right now. If he doesn't like the idea, you can find something else. We can help you choose right now. And you can ask Ms. Calloway to approve it when we're back in class."

She reached across the table and handed him the phone. He took it warily, hesitated for a moment, and then boldly dialed his father's number.

When Jim Eagleson first answered the phone he sounded gruff and angry, but he was surprised, and even pleased, when he realized that it was his son calling. Stumbling and fumbling a bit, Hawk managed to get out the information about the class project. His father asked a few questions, then there was a long pause. Finally, his father said, "Sure, it sounds like a good idea. Just get your teacher's okay, and I can help you with it this weekend."

Hawk thanked him and then, encouraged by his father's tone, quickly told him about their sudden move from the taxi into Selim's room.

"Hmmm.... That's probably for the best," his father said. "One month, huh? Well, hopefully something will happen in one month."

When Hawk handed the phone back to Panny, she gave him a look of mock disappointment. "That's terrible, Hawk-boy. You mean I'll never see your famous live-in taxi?"

Out in the school playground a few of the boys asked Hawk to kick a soccer ball with them. One of them was Charles.

"You don't want to spend all your time with fat boys and oriental chicks, do you?" Charles asked him. Hawk shrank at the insult but decided to join in anyway, if only to show Charles that he wasn't afraid.

They played for a while, and when the bell rang they lined up with the others. Charles said to Hawk, "Let me read your palm, will you?" When Hawk looked baffled, Charles commanded, "Hold out your palm, Princess!" Hawk stuck out his right hand and Charles thrust a folded piece of paper into it. Hawk shoved it in his pocket.

Back in his seat, Hawk pulled out the note and read it: *Bring one dollar on Monday. Otherwise trouble. The Ferret Master.*

The rest of the afternoon was spent in math study — in this case they were dealing with graphing. Ms. Calloway explained that they would combine with a partner to graph multiple intelligences by producing a double bar graph with which each student could compare his or her multiple intelligences to a friend's. But since, according to Ms. Calloway, the existing information forms for multiple intelligences weren't adequate for grade four, they would design their own questionnaires and use them in preparing the information. Then they would make large graphs and demonstrate them to the class.

Hawk set to work with a very cool, slender, dark-eyed girl named Eliza Dean. He figured that one of his "intelligences" was physical, since he played so much baseball, but the others kind of baffled him. He wasn't particularly good at math, no good at music, and what the heck, he wondered, did "interpersonal" mean? His project partner kept trying to get his attention, telling him over and over exactly what he should do. "I like your blond braids," Eliza said. "But you seem to be a bit out of it."

"Piss off!" Hawk told her. The pressures of the day were becoming too much for him. His comment reached the neighbouring desks and some of the kids giggled. Ms. Calloway called Hawk up to her desk.

"Are you having a problem, Hawk? Can I help you?"

"No, I'm all right. It's just that girl — she's too bossy."

"Eliza? Well, I'm sure if you're patient you won't find her so. She probably just wants to help you. Why don't you try again?"

"Okay. But Ms. Calloway, what does *interpersonal* mean? I don't know if I've got it or not."

Ms. Calloway smiled. "Well, I'll tell you, Hawk. You just go back to your desk and try to get along with Eliza. And if you succeed, then you can assume you've got interpersonal intelligence."

Hawk returned to work. Eliza seemed amused. He continued to find her bossy, but he gritted his teeth and bore it. After a while she seemed to loosen up, and to consult him before she plunged ahead, and he began to like her better. He enjoyed what they were doing, and the afternoon passed more quickly.

The day ended with some free time for those kids who had completed their work and had no homework due. "You can have free time today, too, Hawk," Ms. Calloway told him. "But in the future you'll have to earn it. For the next fifteen minutes you can work at anything that interests you."

Hawk moved off to one of the computers and began to surf the Web. He looked up Babe Ruth and found more information about the missing baseball. He felt badly that he couldn't be right there with Mr. Rizzuto, helping to dig out more information on those baseball games of long ago. He might not be as great at research as the kids in his new class, but he was sure he would learn fast. He might even find some important clues that would lead them to that missing baseball.

Hawk was eager to talk to Mr. Rizzuto, but had begun to wonder if his older friend was pursuing what his father would have called a pipe dream. If only he had more time, Hawk felt, he would be able to make that dream a reality, or at least to help find the truth. But he was so busy, and things were happening so fast, he could barely keep up with it all.

Hawk decided that as soon as he had told his mother some reassuring things about how his day had gone he would head off to afternoon baseball practice. This was the day he and Martin would challenge Elroy and see if they could get him stirred up and afraid, so that he would lead them at last to the Rippers. It was an exciting thought, a bit scary, but it might help him get his glove back. Then he wouldn't have to worry about this crazy school stuff. He could play baseball, get on the Little League team, and maybe help find Babe Ruth's baseball before anyone else did!

Before he left the room, however, Ms. Calloway took him aside and explained a bit more about his project. It needn't be on medieval studies, she told him, since he had missed all the classes on that subject. But it had to be on a par with the others. She explained exactly what she wanted, and handed him a written set of instructions.

"If you have any questions, talk to me or to Ms. Clarke," she explained. "You'll meet Ms. Clarke tomorrow, and I know you'll like her. You come up with a project and we'll talk about it then. We're eager to have you succeed and do your best with us, Hawk. We believe in your abilities. This class is going to be a big turning point for you."

Chapter 11

Scaring Elroy

Hawk headed home after school, but his mother was nowhere to be found. He fetched the key for their room from the restaurant, went in and changed clothes, then took off for the practice field. He left a note for Storm Cloud: *School was fine. I'm playing ball. Might have to go to Dad's tonight or tomorrow.*

Hawk jogged through the Riverdale streets, eager to get to the practice field. The sky had turned overcast, a sharp wind blew bits of paper and cast-off coffee cups along the sidewalk. Hawk shivered and kept on moving. Images from the day at school flashed through his mind — they weren't all bad, but already there was almost too much pressure on him. The other kids seemed to take everything in stride, but he was different. He was the one who'd been living first in a taxi, and now a restaurant, the kid who'd been held up and robbed by the Rippers gang, the kid who had latched on to the dream of finding a magic baseball that the great Babe Ruth had once hit for a home run. He was the Grade Four kid who had to take on a school project halfway through the year and try to match the work of the brightest kids in the city.

For an instant he felt weighed down, helpless, but minutes later, when he was at his gloomiest, his most doubtful, he suddenly remembered something his father had told him a couple of years before. He had been feeling hopeless about something, and Jim had taken him aside and told him that he should have more courage. Everyone, but kids in particular, Jim said, had a secret talisman, a magic power in their deepest souls — it was something intangible but so real that you could sense it and feel it, even if you only half tried. Once you located that power, if you made sure to stay in touch with it, held it firmly in your mind and body, you could overcome most of the bad things that life would throw at you. It was just a matter of not giving in, of not cutting yourself off from your own strength by feeling sorry for yourself, or forcing yourself to be something that was wrong for you. Those things would put out your inner light, kill your inner strength.

Hawk had forgotten his dad's exact words, but he remembered the message: *find the power in yourself, believe in it! Be a warrior!* And now, as he walked along these very ordinary streets in Riverdale, suddenly, under a cold, dull sky everything changed. Out of nowhere — or so it seemed — he felt a rush of energy, a stirring of power in his chest, arms, and legs. Just like that, in a twinkling, he was strong, safe in his own skin, and in touch with himself. It was as if the wind had forced him to stand tall, while at the same time it filled his lungs with fresh air, good feelings. He would do the class paper; he would deal with that creepy Charles and the Ferrets. If anyone could find Babe Ruth's baseball, he could. Nothing could hurt him. Lightheartedly, he laughed and ran down the street toward the baseball lot.

"You look great, Hawk," Mr. Rizzuto told him, as the boy approached the field and shouted a greeting. "School agrees with you." The old man glanced up at the sky. "And we're getting some sunshine at last. Maybe you brought it with you?"

Mr. Rizzuto was hauling some equipment out of his van, with the help of the boy from Chile and the two girls. "And here's Martin just coming along," he added. "Maybe he'll go back to school, too. It didn't hurt *you* none, I see. Here, Hawk, wanna help drag this batting cage over there for me?"

Hawk started to struggle with the heavy cage. Then Martin suddenly appeared, mumbled a greeting, and lent a hand with the wire monster. "I don't see Elroy," he said. "I hope he doesn't skip today."

"We moved out of the taxi," Hawk told him. "Panny thinks the Rippers figured out that I was after Elroy. They threw a rock at the Oldsmobile and Mr. Selim, the restaurant owner, took us in. I hope Elroy shows up today. The gang may have warned him not to."

"Maybe," Martin said tersely. "But look, here he comes. I guess he's got more guts than we thought."

Sure enough, Elroy was trudging along from the direction of the railway yards, a bat over his shoulder and a glove swinging on the end of it like a flag on a pole.

Hawk and Martin eyed him slyly as they finished putting the cage in place. Sunlight flashed on the empty lot. The Contreras boys came out from behind a long line of cars. Two other boys tagged along behind.

"Busy day," Martin said. "Don't forget, we've got to lean on Elroy. Tricky thing to do with everyone here."

"We'll get him alone in the outfield," Hawk said.

"This is great!" Mr. Rizzuto called out. "A great squad! Let's set up an infield practice."

He herded them together and starting passing out equipment and shouting instructions. The Contreras boys he directed to short and third. Their friends, two brothers from Mexico, and one of the girls he sent to the outfield. "You're playing in," he told them, "to make a play at the plate."

Martin was at bat, the other girl the pitcher, and the Chilean boy was crouched behind the plate. "Hawk, you play second," Mr. Rizzuto ordered. "And Elroy, first." They nodded and moved off, but before they'd taken more than a few steps, Mr. Rizzuto shouted, "Hey, Elroy, I thought you had a first baseman's glove!"

Elroy stopped, turned, and looked first at Mr.

Rizzuto then at Hawk. "Oh, I lent that to someone," he explained. He spoke very softly. "But that's all right, I can use my outfielder's glove today."

"Okay, okay, if you have to! Get down there then!"

Hawk was stunned. Elroy had hidden or ditched the glove. Or maybe the Rippers had gotten worried and taken it back. Now what would they do? He wanted badly to talk to Martin, but just then it was impossible.

The practice started. Martin hit a few balls to the infield. The Contreras boys did their usual razzle-dazzle and Hawk managed to snare a line drive. He tossed the ball to Elroy who caught it without looking at him. They played in various combinations, then finally Mr. Rizzuto changed them around, and Martin, Hawk, and Elroy found themselves in the outfield.

This was Hawk's big chance. It was time for the scare tactics. He called out to the Southern boy, just loud enough for him to hear, "Hey, Elroy, what happened to my glove? Have you hidden it somewhere?"

Elroy hardly looked at him. "What you goin' on about? I ain't got your glove.... And I don't have to talk to you."

"You prefer to talk to your friends? Maybe to that Ringo? He's a great guy. Is he the one who gave you my glove — the one he stole from me?"

"I ain't sayin' nothin' about nothin'. I'm here to play ball."

"We want to have a chat with you sometime, Elroy. Me and my friends," Hawk said. "Otherwise you'll be in big trouble."

"I ain't worried about no trouble from you," Elroy said.

Hawk tried a few more times to rouse him, to stir him up, but Elroy hung tough. He clamped his mouth shut and said nothing. While the practice continued — another forty-five minutes — he avoided both Hawk and Martin, and when Mr. Rizzuto started wrapping things up, Elroy quickly took his leave.

When he had walked off and disappeared into the next street, Martin started after him.

"Good luck. And be careful!" Hawk whispered to his friend. He then turned back to help Mr. Rizzuto pack up. The other kids gradually disappeared in different directions, and the old man and the boy were left alone.

"So, school went well on your first day?" Mr. Rizzuto asked. "That's good, Hawk. You'll be pretty busy these days with that stuff, but don't forget we're partners, and we're going to find that famous Babe ball."

"I hope so. That Mr. Wingate — he doesn't have any news yet?"

"Not yet. But don't worry. He'll do his job. We'll probably find out something next week. You still on board, kid?"

"I sure am!"

Mr. Rizzuto gave him a glance. "Yeah, I believe you. You look a lot more with it today, Hawk. Something good happened, I guess. You went to see your dad?"

"I did. But something else happened, too. It's great news. We finally moved out of that taxi! The bad news is that somebody threw a rock at the car and broke a window. We had to get out of there. Mr. Selim gave us a room at the back of his restaurant — it's only for a month, but we're safe there."

Mr. Rizzuto waved him into the van. "That's good news — great news," he said, slamming the back doors. He climbed in, started the engine, and they pulled away. "You know," he told Hawk, "I think some good things are going to happen. Just remember, a month is a long time."

"Yeah." Hawk smiled. "That's what my dad said."

Mr. Rizzuto drove Hawk back to Selim's. When he saw the yard and the big empty space where the Oldsmobile had been rotting and rusting away all those years, he shook his head and whistled softly. "Holy cow! I wonder where they took that monster. Not worth much, even for scrap. But, boy, I'm sure glad you're out of there!"

Hawk started to run inside, but turned back. "Hey, Mr. Rizzuto. Don't forget to tell me what that Mr. Wingate finds out."

"Don't worry, kid! You'll be the first to know."

Hawk waved goodbye, slipped through the back door, and found Storm Cloud coming out to meet him. "So here you are!" she said, sounding a bit cross. "I got your note. And your dad left a message with Mr. Selim. He wants you to go over there tonight to study with him. You're supposed to give a talk on Native customs, he told me, in your class.

Well, that's okay. That's just great. But you could have asked me for some help, too." She frowned and pushed Hawk gently toward the door of their room. "I know almost as much about the subject as he does."

Chapter 12

Bad News from Martin

Hawk went to school the next day thinking of his father's great stories about the origins of their people, the Ojibway and Cree, who had lived all across eastern North America before and after the coming of the white settlers. Jim had spent the evening describing the difficult but wonderful life of these tribes, and the natural environment of woods and lakes in which they flourished. He offered Hawk some chocolate milk and they ate chicken sandwiches. A recording of Native drumming sounded in the background.

The evening passed quickly. Hawk's brain whirled with images of sunlight on shining lakes, snow-dusted teepees, birchbark canoes, sacred scrolls, sun dance ceremonies, and burial mounds. His father promised to tell him more about these and other wonders, each in its turn. Hawk found everything magical. It was true that his mother had explained some things about the Ojibway traditions, and these were mostly accurate, but despite her claim, his father knew much more. Besides, he was a great storyteller.

"I think I'm learning a lot, don't you, Dad? I think I can do a great class presentation," Hawk said, as his father prepared to take him home.

"I hope so," his father said. "Don't be overconfident, but stay in touch with that strong light within you."

Lining up for class, Hawk did feel in touch with something strong in himself. Even the sneering face of Charles, head of the Ferrets, didn't frighten him, or make him anxious.

Several kids clustered around Charles, and Hawk noticed one of them, a small, curly-haired boy, passing him a small envelope. That kid must be paying his dues. Hawk felt his anger rise, but controlled it. He wouldn't become one of those Ferret flunkies!

When he entered the classroom, Ms. Calloway was busy in front of the blackboard posters, talking and consulting bulky files and a laptop computer with another woman. Catching sight of Hawk, she signalled him to come up.

"This is your other teacher, Hawk. Meet Ms. Clarke. We work together, although we mostly teach on different days." She nodded at her partner, a slim woman with straight auburn hair and penetrating blue eyes. "I've already suggested that Hawk jump right in and do a research project."

"Sounds great. Have you decided what the topic is?" Ms. Clarke asked.

Hawk gulped, but answered promptly. "I want to do something on the Ojibway-Cree Nations, to tell the class about their history and customs. My dad is helping me. He's an expert. He works for the Native Centre."

The teachers exchanged glances. "That sounds terrific," Ms. Calloway said. "I hear you're a great reader, so you should be able to find lots of information in the library, and on the Web. But there's no substitute for your dad's experience."

"You should bring us a draft," Ms. Clarke said. "Ms. Calloway or I can look it over and tell you if you're on the right track. I hope you do really well in this class, Hawk. I'll be teaching science, math, gym, and music mostly, and Ms. Calloway will handle art, literature, and social studies. But we both do everything. So if you have any questions, just ask one of us."

"Maybe you could have the draft by next week," Ms. Calloway suggested. "By the way, your dad is Jim Eagleson, isn't he? I heard him give a talk last year — it was very good. I learned a lot about Wee-sa-kay-jac, the trickster in the Cree stories. You know the Greeks and the Norse had trickster figures in their stories, as well. Too bad you missed that part of our class,

Hawk. But don't worry. You can catch up on a lot. Now enjoy the day with Ms. Clarke. There's science and gym today, which I'm sure you'll like."

For most of the morning until recess they worked at geological studies, and rock collections came into play, charts showing varieties of rock formations, regions, and sites of origin, and the way rocks figured in architecture, sculpture, temple-building, and worship. When the bell rang and they lined up to go outside, Charles came up behind Hawk, bumped him, making it seem like an accident, and slipped something into his pocket. In the schoolyard, Hawk dodged away from Panny and Albert and cast a quick glance at what Charles had palmed on him. It was a small cardboard picture about half the size of a playing card that showed, in black and white, a sneering image of a skull and crossbones. A single word had been written in red ink under the crossed bones: *MONDAY*.

Hawk shuddered despite himself. Panny ran over and joined him, Albert puffing along behind. "Hey, you okay?" she asked Hawk. "You know I'm worried about Martin. I haven't heard a thing from him. He was supposed to track down Elroy, remember? If I don't get a message by the time school's out, I'm going to start to really worry. Everything okay with that project idea?"

"Sure, the teachers liked it. And my dad is teaching me lots of things. I know I can do it."

For the rest of the day, Hawk tried to concentrate on his work, but it was difficult. The skull-and-crossbones card seemed to radiate bad vibes from his pocket, upsetting his train of thought. He knew he ought to talk to his teachers about it, but right now he was scared to do it. He would talk to Panny first. Maybe she could help him get in touch with his inner strength.

At the end of the day, Ms. Clarke led them through gym class. "She's great," Panny whispered. "She can do a double cartwheel."

At first they played dodge ball, and then Ms. Clarke appointed a student leader and an assistant. They conferred and made up a game for the class to play. It was a complicated game with ropes, bars, and basketballs. Some of the kids complained about the rules. "All right," Ms. Clarke said to the two leaders, "now you have to resolve the situation. Either make your rules clearer or change them." The leaders conferred and came up with a revision that the class liked. Hawk was keen on the game. At one point he tossed a ball very hard and hit Charles in the back. It was an accident. The other boy approached him slowly. His glance was dark-eyed, dangerous. He gave Hawk a slight, covert shove, and said, "Monday!"

When the final bell sounded at last, Panny came up to Hawk and whispered, "I hope you don't mind, but I invited Albert along. I told him what was going on and I thought he could help us out. And in case things go bad, his cousin's a cop, so maybe we could get him to help us, too."

"That's great," Hawk answered, smiling. "The more of us, the better."

Panny signalled to Albert, and the three walked out of the school and took off together in the direction of Chinatown, talking all the way. (To simplify things, Panny had left her bike at home.)

As they walked, Hawk fingered Charles's skull-and-crossbones card in his pocket. He wanted to tell his new friends everything and get their advice, but he just couldn't find the right words.

Panny didn't notice Hawk's discomfort. She had something else on her mind. "I heard from Martin," she said. "It's pretty bad. He followed Elroy, but the gang caught him and he had to run for his life. Our friend sounded pretty shaky. He was a little nervous to come over to Chinatown from his aunt's apartment. That isn't like Martin. Anyway, he wants to meet us at the Schnitzel House Restaurant on Gerrard, near my house. His aunt eats there and he knows the owner, so he feels safe. He's found out something big about the Rippers, but he seemed almost scared to tell me on the phone."

"Martin scared? I can't believe that," Hawk said.

"Who chased him?" Albert asked.

"No idea," Panny said. "We'll find out in a few minutes."

They walked west on the Danforth, then bore south past Withrow Park and headed toward the colourful array of stores that made up Chinatown East. The Schnitzel House seemed out of place here. It was a relic of past times and sat uneasily beside the bustling Asian markets and restaurants like an old aunt watching a lively party that she couldn't quite join. There was something gloomy, and maybe a little grimy about the place, Hawk thought. It smelled of sausages, beer, and noodle soup, and was occupied at that moment by only three or four customers, grey-haired men chatting away in German or Hungarian. They gave the kids a brief, curious glance as they entered.

A bald man in a white apron stepped out of a passageway and greeted the three youngsters. "Hello, you kids are here to see *der Junge* Martin? Good! Come right this way."

He whisked them away down the hall and opened a door to reveal a small private room decorated in faded green and gold. Martin stood smiling by an old oak table. Panny introduced Albert and Martin, then they all sat down. Martin said, "I'm glad you made it. I had a bit of a problem yesterday."

"The Rippers spotted you?" Hawk asked.

"More than that! I followed them down to South Riverdale and hid out in a nearby lot, keeping an eye on the house that Elroy went into. It wasn't that far from the house he lives in — the one we all saw. The gang must have seen me following them, and a couple of them crept up and jumped me. They took me to some warehouse nearby. They made me talk to Ringo. He didn't say much, just kept smiling. It was scary. They asked a lot of questions and lifted my cellphone, but Elroy spoke up for me and I managed to escape."

"Elroy?" Albert asked. "You mean the guy who has Hawk's baseball glove?"

"Yeah. And there were a couple of others besides Ringo there too. Tough teens. They said weird things, like they were going to cut me up, or throw me in the Don River. They asked why I was bugging Elroy, and whether you'd gone to the police about your glove, Hawk. They wanted to know where you'd moved to, because the Oldsmobile was gone from Selim's. I told them I didn't know much about you — I just played baseball with you. I told them you'd pay me if I got your glove back — that's why I was following Elroy."

"But Elroy knew it wasn't just that," Hawk said. "We scared him on the field and accused him of being connected with the Rippers."

"I know, but for some reason — maybe because he doesn't like the Rippers now — he tried to cover for me."

"That's good news," Panny said. "I was pretty sure the Rippers were pressuring him. So how did you get away?"

"Elroy kept telling them they had to let me go. We were in some kind of cellar. Finally he just shoved the door open and told me to run. I took off and ran like hell. They chased me for a block or so, but I got out to some busy street and they gave up."

"I wonder what happened to Elroy?" Hawk asked.

"I don't know. Maybe nothing. They had just had a visit from a guy who must be the big boss. I watched the whole thing. He arrived in a fancy black car with a chauffeur and they treated him like he was the king or something — Mr. Big. That's how they caught me — I got a bit distracted watching, and a couple of them sneaked up on me. Mr. Big was just leaving, just driving away when these young guys, gang members, jumped me. I think Mr. Big was there to meet Elroy, to welcome him to the gang. I think Panny was right about Elroy being used by them. They were trying to impress him. So maybe they didn't care that I got away. I was just some guy who turned up by accident. They figured they could just shoo me away. I don't really think they would have hurt me — but it was scary."

"So this Mr. Big — what did he look like?" Albert asked.

Martin didn't answer. He looked from one to another of his friends, and finally his eyes rested on Panny.

"That's the funny thing. When I called you from my aunt's apartment, Panny, I couldn't quite get this out on the phone, but there was one thing I noticed about Mr. Big — he was a very well-dressed guy, filthy rich, I guess, and he was Asian, maybe Chinese."

Chapter 13

Right Up Panny's Street

They all looked shocked. Then Panny smiled. "I'm not worried. Every group has its problems, right? But how did you know the guy was Chinese? Not all Asians are Chinese!"

Martin smiled. "I know that. I wasn't sure, until I remembered that I'd gone to dim sum with my aunt one time, and I noticed the same guy, or someone who looked an awful lot like him, at another table. He was dressed in a suit and tie and looked different from all the others — important. I was curious, so I asked my aunt about him. She knew the restaurant owner, and he told her the guy was a big shot in the Chinese community, a rich guy who supported a lot of charities. I think the owner didn't want to go into more detail, even though he may have known more."

Panny smiled. "Sure, that's how it goes all right. I guess he thought the less you outsiders knew about the Asian gang scene, the better!"

She winked, laughed, opened the hall door, and pointed the way for the others. "Don't worry! The fact that Mr. Big is Chinese makes it all the easier to check him out. The person we need to see is Professor Sam."

They left the Schnitzel House in a hurry, calling out their thanks to the bald-headed manager. Back on the busy street, Panny gave them instructions. "I'm heading home to get my bike and to pick up Chew-Boy. If you walk two streets east and turn right you'll be on Emerald Avenue. Look for Number 202. That's where Dr. Sam lives." She glanced at her watch. "He should be there right now, but I'll call him on the way just to make sure. See you in about ten minutes! And by the way, don't buy any food. Dr. Sam always has great stuff to eat."

As Panny sprinted away down a side street, the three boys walked on slowly down Gerrard.

"Wow! You think this rich guy really is the head of the Rippers?" Albert asked Martin.

Martin shook his head. "I don't think so. He must be into other things. More important things. He probably just uses the Rippers to do some of his dirty work. I hope they don't beat up Elroy. He can help us."

"I wonder who Dr. Sam is." Hawk said.

"We'll soon find out," Albert replied.

It didn't take the boys long to find 202 Emerald. It was a medium-sized brick apartment block, neat and tidy, with small balconies, some of them decorated with plants and flowers.

They had been killing time hanging around outside the building for only a few minutes when Panny zoomed down the street, red panniers catching the light and a white fluffy animal squirming around in the front basket of her bike.

"He's up there!" she shouted to them. "Second floor. I'll lock my bike in the lobby. Here's Chew-Boy — see how happy he is to be going visiting! He can protect us if we get ambushed."

The boys laughed. The idea of that animated muff protecting anyone seemed pretty doubtful.

"Don't laugh!" Panny said. "Chew-Boy is a real killer."

They laughed again and trooped up the stairs. Panny led them to Apartment 26 and knocked on the door.

"Come in, Panny! It's open," said a clear, bright voice.

They stepped into the apartment, walked down a long book-lined hall, and came out in a big sitting room, a comfortable space that contained more books, a sofa, armchairs, and a work table stacked with computer equipment. The walls were covered with paintings and posters. Some of them were crime posters, police "wanted" notices, and photographs of crime scenes.

A tall, slender man dressed in jeans, a T-shirt,

and low cowboy boots greeted them. He nodded to each of them as the boys were introduced.

"Quite a gang, Panny! They all look pretty smart — must be from your gifted class."

"Right on!" Panny told him. "This is my cousin, Sammy Chang," she explained to the boys. "He's a professor of criminology at York. Knows just about everything you'd want to know — and maybe more — about crime and gangs in Metro Toronto. Usually has some food around, too." She looked at him expectantly.

"Your timing is good, Panny — as usual. Good to see Chew-Boy, too." He laughed and his horn-rimmed glasses, hanging by a string, bobbed up and down on his shirt. He disappeared into the kitchen and they heard some rattling dishes. Hawk and the other boys studied the posters.

"Wow! Look at this one — 'Street gangs of Toronto and area' — I wonder if the Rippers are on here."

"And here's a wanted poster for some serial killer," Albert pointed out. "The Mississauga Strangler. Suspected of thirteen murders. Last seen east of Toronto stuck on a stalled GO train and carrying an orange suitcase."

"He doesn't exist," Panny told them. "My cousin's students made some up for a joke. Oh, boy! That looks good, Dr. Sam!"

The young professor had carried out a large tray weighed down with spring rolls, barbecued pork buns, won ton crackers, chicken wings, and egg tarts. “There’s some orange soda on the counter out there,” he told them.

“Of course you guys realize that you’re eating my supper,” Sammy added, with a wry smile. “But don’t worry. My girlfriend’s just invited me out for Indian food.

“Now, Panny, what’s all this about these gangs you’re scouting? — It’s not something I would recommend, by the way,” he added.

“It’s okay, we’re not being stupid about it,” Panny reassured him. She picked off some chicken from one of the wings and fed it to Chew-Boy. ”We know it’s dangerous stuff to get into, but it wasn’t our fault. The Rippers gang stole a baseball glove from my friend Hawk here. They gave it to a boy named Elroy, and we think they’re using him to do some bad stuff. We just want to get the glove back, get Elroy out of trouble, and pass along the case to Albert’s cousin, who’s with the police. But now Martin here, our main scout, has spotted something unexpected and we thought we’d check it out with you.”

“Very good. So check.”

“Well, you know something about the Chinese gangs in Toronto, right?”

“A few things, sure. It’s one of my specialties.”

“So could there be some Chinese gang that’s using some kid street gang like the Rippers to pull off things, and could that gang be headed by a well-dressed, grey-haired, distinguished-looking Chinese gentleman who gets driven around town in a black limo?”

"That's a blue suit for the gentleman," Martin cut in. "And the car is an old Cadillac or Lincoln, or something like that — but in great condition."

Professor Sam considered this. "Wow! That's a pretty general description. It isn't going to help the police very much if they have to look for these guys. I probably can't identify this fellow you've seen, Martin, or tell you for sure if he's connected to the Rippers. Tell you what, I'll just fill you in on the Chinese gang scene, and then, if you think there may be a connection, you can go to the police. But before I tell you anything, you're going to have to promise not to take on this crowd by yourselves. I don't care if you do hang out in a gifted class — this could be dangerous territory!"

"Sure, we all agree to that, don't we, boys?" Panny glanced around her circle and each of her friends nodded. The professor saw this and continued.

"Okay. First of all, I should mention triads. This is a special Chinese idea. It goes way back to the eighteenth century and was the basis of some secret patriotic societies of the time. The sign used by these societies was the triangle, or triad, the three-way connection of heaven, Earth, and humans. Over time these triad societies became criminal organizations. When China was ruled by the Maoist Communists, these societies tended to work from Hong Kong, which was still under British rule. From there the gangs spread out to wherever Chinese people settled.... Now, you know, these gangs are secret and they demand loyalty from their members. They may not threaten every individual, but they can be like bullies in the schoolyard. If they notice you and you don't co-operate with them, or if you try to stand up against them, you can get into big trouble."

Hawk felt his throat go dry. He squeezed the already crumpled skull-and-crossbones card in his pocket. Gangs and bullies, secret societies. But his father had taught him that he, too, was a warrior. A good warrior. He had to keep in touch with the fire inside him.

At this point, Albert raised his hand.

"A question?" Dr. Sam asked. "Fire away! Or maybe I shouldn't put it like that when we're talking about gangs!"

Albert and the others laughed.

"Is it something like the Mafia?" Albert asked.

"Good question, Albert. Yes, it is, with some big differences, of course. Now, the triads have operated in Canada for some time — there must be at least eight to ten thousand members across the country. They do lots of nasty things, and they're a great embarrassment to the Chinese community. The triad gangs here have their specialties. They do a lot of counterfeiting and credit card theft and forgery. They deal with illegal movies and DVDs and stuff like that. They smuggle specimens of endangered species. Not to mention car theft, gambling, drugs — and many other nasty things that make them a lot of money."

At this point Hawk raised his hand. He was so excited he could hardly speak, but he managed to get control of himself. "Excuse me, Dr. Sam. Could these triads also deal with sports souvenirs? I mean, could they forge things like autographs and signed pictures and hockey cards and stuff like that?"

The professor slipped off his glasses and let them hang on their string, then began to push them back and forth in front of him as he spoke.

"Definitely! I can see you kids are from a gifted class. These criminals go with the flow, Hawk. They find or steal what the market wants. There are lots of people in Canada who collect sports mementos and souvenirs. So why not forge them and make some money?"

Hawk remembered what Mr. Rizzuto had told him: *There are a whole lot of forgers and guys who peddle counterfeit stuff. They make money from their swindles so they can afford big prices to buy real authentic stuff.*

Of course, that Babe Ruth baseball would be just the kind of thing they'd go for! And hadn't Mr. Rizzuto been told that "others" were paying Mr. Wingate for special information on Toronto and the islands?

Hawk squirmed in his seat and wondered if Mr. Big was connected to more than his stolen glove. It was really important that they get in touch with Elroy and convince him to help them out.

Then Panny said, "Thanks, Dr. Sam. Great information. Up until now, all I knew about the triads was that their members had to swear funny oaths, like 'If I rob a sworn brother I will be killed by five thunderbolts!' But what do you think? Could this Chinese guy that Martin saw be connected to the Rippers? Could the Rippers really be working with a triad gang?"

The professor shrugged his shoulders. "Anything's possible, cousin Panny," he said. "If there's big money in there somewhere, there could some gang stuff involved, Chinese or otherwise. The Rippers might just be the lowest rung on the ladder. Which is all the more reason for you kids to stay clear of it. I don't want either the Rippers or the Sun Yee On, or anybody else for that matter, to come around and give any of you a good spanking!"

At that instant, Chew-Boy stood up and barked. They all jumped, hearts in their throats, and seconds later burst out laughing.

"I hope that isn't a bad omen," the professor said. "Anybody want another egg tart?"

Chapter 14

Kids on the Warpath, Slowly

Outside on the street, the kids went over their plans.

"So, Professor Sam doesn't want us to go after that gang," Albert said. "I guess we'd better take his advice, right, Panny?"

Panny looked thoughtful, but Martin frowned and spoke up with passion. "After all our trouble?" he protested. "Just to let the gang get away with it? No way!"

"We don't want to end up in the Don River," Albert said. "And besides, the police won't like it, and our parents will kill us if the criminals don't!"

"Nobody's going to kill us," Panny assured him. "Look, boys, it's only Friday. Albert and I have very busy Saturdays. I have music lessons and Chinese school, and he has chess and art classes. And I'll bet Hawk here has some more studying to do with his dad. So let's do it this way. We don't rush off right now or tomorrow. We meet on Sunday morning outside of Elroy's house. It has to be early, in case his mum makes him go to church. From what Martin says, we should be able to convince him to help us. At the very least we might get him to break with the gang. When we hear what he says, we can decide what to do. Either we go to the police or we try something ourselves ... or maybe a little of both! How about it, guys?"

Hawk nodded enthusiastically. He was anxious to see his dad. Monday, the deadline set by Charles, the Ferret Master, was coming around fast. He just couldn't tell the kids about the Ferrets, although he was bursting to. They were all working together to get his glove back, to help Elroy — and now maybe there was a connection with Mr. Big and the lost Babe Ruth baseball. He couldn't dump his Ferret problem on them, too — they might even laugh at him. No, he would get advice from his dad about that one. He had real respect from his friends and he wanted to keep it. And he trusted his dad so much more now.

"Should we meet behind the Dumpsters opposite Elroy's house?" he asked.

"Right, Hawk," Panny agreed. "Let's make it nine o'clock. We'll figure out how to get hold of Elroy without his mum being around when we size up the scene. Just call me if anything comes up between now and then, okay?"

They all agreed and split up right there, scattering in various directions. Hawk headed east toward Mr. Selim's restaurant. He would check in with his mum and then go on to his father's. Jim had promised to meet him at his house around seven. He would stay there overnight and finish up his studies on Saturday. He was due to give Ms. Calloway an outline of his talk on Monday morning. If only the Ferrets weren't threatening him it would all work out so well!

When he got to Mr. Selim's he was surprised to find that his mother wasn't there. Their dusty little room had a funny feel to it, as if it was especially empty and vacant at that moment. Then he noticed that his mother's old suitcase was gone, along with most of her meagre stash of clothing. There was no note, so he ran in search of Mr. Selim.

Hawk found him in the big steaming kitchen that smelled of curry, baked nan, and tandoori chicken. A young Indian man, busy tending stewpots and ovens according to Selim's instructions, winked at Hawk.

"Ah, young man!" Mr. Selim smiled at him. "I have a message for you from your mother. I'm glad you're here because she was rather frantic to find you before she left. She had to leave suddenly, you see, because a lady friend of hers came with a car to take her to Ottawa. A 'once-in-a-lifetime chance,' your good mother said. So she made me promise to find you and tell you to go on to your father's house as planned, and stay there for the weekend. She'll telephone him along the way and explain everything. I am so relieved that you made it easy for me!"

Hawk nodded. He felt worried about his mother, and nervous about her plans. Did this mean she was getting ready to take him to Ottawa with her? His dad had said he didn't have to go, and Hawk hoped his dad would get his way. He was sad that his mother was leaving Riverdale, but he sure didn't want to move to Ottawa with her.

"Bring your dad to eat here some time," Mr. Selim said, shaking hands with Hawk and turning back to his kitchen supervision.

Hawk packed his clothes and schoolbooks into a small knapsack and hurried out of the restaurant, through the back lot, then down the long side street that connected with the main thoroughfare. There the traffic swarmed and buzzed, as if everyone, fed up with the long work week, was pushing into the weekend as fast as possible.

Hawk ran, heading straight for The Pocket and his father's house, and got there before his dad arrived home. He sat breathless on the back steps, watching the busybody in the house behind the back fence shake her head and mumble to herself, looking quite upset that he appeared to be locked out of his father's house and was just sitting idly there.

It wasn't long before his father arrived, looking pensive. But he quickly brightened up when he saw his son sitting there on the steps. Hawk noticed that his father often had to pull himself out of his blue moods, to escape from whatever thoughts were preoccupying him, before he could focus on just being there with his son. But Hawk had also decided, some time before, that what really mattered was that his father always made the effort to connect with him. That was the good thing; that was what made Hawk happy.

Soon they had settled down to sandwiches and study. Hawk had to answer a lot of questions about what they had studied already: *What were the main divisions of the Ojibway-Cree Nation? What geographical areas did they occupy? What was the relation of their nation to the Iroquois Federation? How were young men initiated into the tribe? What were some of the main totem figures? What was the Medewin Medicine Society? What form did the sacred scrolls take?*

Hawk answered all these questions in detail. He loved learning about the past, especially that of his people, and he wanted to please his father. He was also determined to give a good presentation to his class. When there was a pause in the questioning and Hawk saw how pleased Jim was with his new knowledge, he decided the time had come to talk about his problem with the Ferrets. "Dad, there's something I've got to tell you about my new class," he began.

The story was harder to get out than he had expected. He stumbled a few times, hesitated, and found himself close to tears. But his father's strong eyes held him steady.

"Go ahead, son," Jim said. "Just tell it like it is."

Hawk told him about Charles and his messages and threats — the skull and crossbones, the Monday deadline — and how he didn't know who else might be in the gang. Albert? Maybe even Panny? He put on a brave face, trying to conceal from his father how scared he was, but he knew he hadn't fooled Jim for a moment.

"That little twerp really called you Pocahontas?" his father asked, with a disgusted smile. He shook his head. "Needs a good kick in the butt, that's what he needs. But don't worry about your friends, son. From what you've told me about them, you can be sure they're not part of it! No, I'll tell you exactly what's going to happen. I'm going over to see Ms. Calloway before school on Monday. You're going to tell Panny and Albert about this and go to Ms. Calloway with them. I suspect little Charlie-pants-bully is going to have some explaining to do to his teachers and his parents before that day is out!"

Hawk felt a rush of relief come over him at his father's words. The rest of the evening they spent watching a movie, *Ivanhoe*, about the adventures of a Saxon knight in the Middle Ages. It had some great moments, and Hawk especially liked the scenes that showed the storming of a castle and a big tournament. His dad enjoyed the movie, too.

The next day they went to the zoo, and Hawk saw the lions and tigers and learned the Native names of some of the North American animals. Later, they played baseball in the backyard, with the old lady behind the fence glaring at them the whole time.

That night, Hawk was restless. He was eager to see Panny, Albert, and Martin the next day, but was glad that he hadn't heard any bad news from them. Everything must still be on. He had explained to his father that he wanted to meet the boys early, fibbing that they were going to Chinatown for dim sum with Panny.

"Well, you can set the alarm and go," Jim had said. "Just be back here in the afternoon. This will be a good chance for you to tell your friends about Charles and his nonsense. I know they'll back you up one hundred percent."

Hawk nodded. He felt badly that he couldn't tell his father what was really happening — about the Rippers, about Panny's idea of splitting Elroy from the gang and helping him, and about the gang connections between the Rippers and Mr. Big. But he knew that if he did tell him, Jim wouldn't let him go.

He tossed and turned in his bed for a while, but finally dozed off. The next thing he knew, the alarm was blaring in his ear. He turned it off and crawled out of bed. It was morning and he was ready for his Sunday adventure.

Chapter 15

Closing in on the Gangs

It was a sunny Sunday, getting warm fast, and the streets were still pretty empty of traffic. Hawk had been too excited to eat before he left, so by the time he had trudged through the just-waking city and got to South Riverdale he was starving.

Luckily, a few blocks away from Elroy's house Panny came zooming up the street, greeted him, and pulled a couple of bags of food out of her overstuffed panniers. They sat on the steps of an old deserted warehouse and Hawk dug into the food.

"I thought you might be hungry — and the two other guys even left something for you. They're watching the house already from behind the dumpster. How did your time with your dad go?"

"It was great." Hawk gave her a shy look, hesitating. "But I have to tell you guys something.

It's about school."

"I hope it's not bad. Your dad's not pulling you out of our class, is he?"

"No. It's something that happened. But maybe I could eat first."

Hawk started stuffing himself with the cold shrimp shumai, won ton chips, and pork dumplings that Panny handed over. "Here, have some orange juice, too," she told him with a smile. "Don't want you choking to death before I hear your big secret."

Hawk swigged some of the orange juice and without a pause began rattling off his story to Panny. She sat there, wide-eyed, listening to his account of Charles's bullying tactics, and, as he concluded, he mentioned his Monday "deadline." Panny jumped to her feet, wheeled her bicycle up and down in a frantic motion, and said, "Ms. Calloway will soon put a stop to that!"

When she had calmed down a little, she added, "I'm surprised that we didn't hear about all that stuff. Of course I knew that some kids hung around Charles, but I didn't know he was a little fascist leader. I thought they were just taken in by his fake cool. Poor Hawk, I'm sorry for you. I'm glad your dad's going in tomorrow. We'll all talk to Ms. Calloway and Ms. Clarke about this. It's just the kind of thing our teachers hate most — bullying. They hate it even more than they hate smart kids who don't cheer for others and are 'all about me'!"

Hawk felt a great wave of relief and was suddenly lighthearted and happy. He almost wanted to get up and dance around. He had friends who would help him, and teachers who could protect him. He walked beside Panny, a smile on his face, as she pushed her bike in the direction of the narrow street that led to Elroy's house.

"Nothing happening so far in the house with the brown curtains," she told Hawk. "Not a car moving on that street yet. The printer's shop is closed, of course, and so is the showroom. It was smart to come down here and catch Elroy on a Sunday. Let's just hope he gets out of the house alone at some point and his mum doesn't drag him off somewhere."

"To church, for example," Hawk said. "Remember, he's from the South and they go to church a lot down there."

"Well, we'll just have to pray that he doesn't," Panny said, giggling. "I brought Chew-Boy, by the way. He's guarding Albert and Martin right now."

They turned down the bleak, empty street and Hawk caught sight of Elroy's house, looking smaller and more desolate than he remembered. More paint seemed to have peeled away and the porch appeared to sag even more than it had a few days before. Across from the house, the Dumpster looked forlorn and deserted.

"The guys are hiding out — that's good," Panny said. "And here's Chew-Boy, wondering where I was all this time."

The small, fluffy, white ball of energy raced toward them, trailing a long leash behind him. Panny jumped off her bike, swept the dog into her arms, and gave him a brief kiss. When she put him back down he pranced up and down for a minute, then followed along happily as she led the way to where they boys were hiding.

They were seated on a small piece of plastic sheeting, their backs resting against two big knapsacks. They had cellphones in hand and were immersed in playing some kind of video game.

"Just what I like to see," Panny scoffed. "Our super-spies watching the house for Elroy's every move. He could be back in Jacksonville by now for all you'd know!"

Martin grunted and got to his feet. "Don't worry, Panny. We've been looking over there every minute or so. It's as quiet as a graveyard. We had enough trouble keeping Chew-Boy from following you. When I heard your voices just now, I let him go."

"One sure thing is that we won't be seeing any of the Rippers this morning," Albert said. "They're probably all still in bed … which is where I'd like to be, too." He yawned and stretched and peered around the Dumpster at the house across the street. "Got any more shumai, Panny?"

"Nothing left!" she answered, and proceeded to tell them about Hawk's troubles at school with the bully, Charles.

Martin and Albert shook their heads in disgust, but before they could say anything, Panny reminded them all why they were there. "Sure, Charles is a snake, but first things first. It's almost 9:30. If Elroy comes out with his mum, I'm going to follow them. I'm the only one he hasn't met, so I can track them without being suspected. Then, when I see a chance to split the boy from his mum so we can talk to him, I'll text you."

"Let's hope something happens soon," Martin said. "After being captured by the Rippers once, I'm not finding spying like this too comfortable."

They settled down and waited, a little restless but conserving their energy as best they could. They had no idea what they might have to do in the next few hours.

After what seemed ages, and when they were almost ready to try something bolder, like going up to the house and knocking on the door themselves, something finally happened.

A low gasp from Albert, who was watching the house at that moment, brought them all to attention.

"Two old ladies," he said. "Heading out somewhere."

"And one of them is Elroy's mother," Hawk said. "I recognize her."

Two older black women, well-dressed in dark colours and wearing old-fashioned Sunday hats, had stepped out on to the porch. They stood chatting for a moment and then strolled off together toward the main street.

"It's church for sure," Albert said. "Now, if Elroy is smart, he'll still be in bed."

"We'll give him half an hour," Panny said. "Then we'll go over and get him."

The three boys gaped at her.

"You weren't planning to wait here all day, were you?" she challenged them.

But they didn't have to go over, and they didn't have to wait very long. Five minutes later the front door opened and a sleepy-eyed Elroy, stretching his arms and yawning, came out on the porch and stood for a minute looking up and down the street.

"Remember our plan," Panny whispered. "Two in each direction to cut him off. You say he's a fast runner, so we've got to block off his escape."

"Maybe he'll just pull out a gun and kill us," Albert said.

"Are you serious?" Panny said. "This is Elroy, not that Ringo freak. He helped Martin to escape, remember? And he'll soon see that we're the best thing that could have happened to him."

"Look! He's starting to move," Martin said.

"And so are we," said Panny. "Martin and Hawk, you try to cut him off. Albert and I will block this end of the street."

Hawk sprinted away, out into the narrow street, Martin right beside him. They ran right past Elroy, turning to block his path. Elroy stopped in his tracks.

"Hey, Elroy!" Martin shouted. "We just want to talk to you."

Elroy turned around and began to jog the other way, but not too fast. "Ain't got nothin' to say!" he shouted back. Suddenly he stopped, spotting Panny and Albert walking toward him on the sidewalk, barring his way.

"What's this gang you got after me?" He turned again and speeded up. He was capable of outrunning them, but had hesitated too long, Hawk and Martin wouldn't let him pass, and the Southern boy reversed his direction suddenly, trying to evade them. He was cutting back across the street, heading for an empty lot, when a small streak of dog, a white muff in motion, caught him and began to nip at his feet.

"Okay, Chew-Boy, don't bite him! Come back, Chew-Boy!" Panny ran up and the dog leapt away. Elroy stood in his tracks, glaring at them. Martin came up and took hold of him.

"We don't want to hurt you, Elroy. I just wanted to thank you for yesterday."

Elroy shook himself free. "I don't need no thanks. I didn't want anyone to get hurt, that's all."

They stood around him, trying hard to reassure him. Panny reached out, shook Elroy's hand, and introduced herself and Chew-Boy.

"Pretty wicked dog," Elroy said. "Tore a hole in one of my socks."

"We'll buy you new ones," Panny assured him. "We just want to talk. Can we sit on one of those iron benches over there?" She pointed to some junk metal in a nearby lot.

"Come over to my house," Elroy said. "We can talk there, but you gotta be quick. My mom will come back from church and maybe some of them Rippers will stop by later."

Chapter 16

Elroy in Trouble

The group followed Elroy back to the old white house with the sagging porch. Inside, he led the way down a dark hallway, one that smelled of cigarettes, hot spices, and burnt coffee. Then into an apartment, dingy, but clean-looking, with some modern furniture and a good-sized television. There was a small, beat-up piano pushed against the far wall, with some music sheets set up on it.

"You play?" Panny asked, pointing to the instrument.

"My mom's teaching me," Elroy said. "I'm catching on a little."

He led them into a small bedroom. Baseball posters covered one wall — Jeter, A-Rod, Jackie Robinson, and a team shot of the Tampa Bay Rays. There was a map of the world on another wall, a full bookcase, and a table with a laptop, a cellphone, MP3 player, and other assorted electronics.

Hawk glanced at the rumpled bed and shivered. His baseball glove — *it must be his!* — lay there beside a bat with a chipped, nearly split handle.

Elroy caught his look, frowned, then walked to the bed and retrieved the glove. He turned it over in his hands, then passed it directly to Hawk. "Here, you take this. I know it's yours. I didn't steal it, but it has caused me nothin' but trouble. I don't need it. I got another one of my own."

Hawk was speechless, and Panny gave him a big smile. To Elroy, she said, "That's a smart thing to do. But you can be even smarter and get yourself out of big trouble. Just tell us what you know about the Rippers."

Elroy shook his head and cast her a doubtful look. "You guys? What can you do? You can't take on them Rippers. You just better grab that glove and get outta here."

But Panny would have none of it. "We didn't come for the glove, Elroy. We're here to help you. You've got to split with that gang. You've got to help us get the police on them."

Elroy said nothing. He sat down on the bed and put his head in his hands. "I can't split with them. That Ringo creeps me out." He went on in a low voice, not looking at them. "He's a killer, that Ringo, or near so. Now they got me to meet that Mr. Big, some Chinese guy who runs some of the worst gangs. Martin saw that. Martin tried to help me. But I can't cross those guys anymore. If I do, I'm done and cooked for sure. I'm a dead boy if I don't play along."

Panny looked around the room at the other kids. She was silent a moment, then she said, "Elroy isn't exaggerating. We know that, don't we?" She went and sat down on the bed beside him and spoke to him in a very quiet voice. "We can help you, Elroy. We just need some information. We need to know more about what the gang's told you, and about Mr. Big. Nobody will know what you passed on to us. They won't even know we met. Just think, it's your only way of getting free of this gang. When the police catch them they'll be way too busy trying to stay out of jail to think of you. You can go on and play baseball, just like you want to. You'll be out of this nightmare."

Elroy pulled his hands away from his face. He sat up straight and looked at Panny, who had picked up Chew-Boy and was holding the dog in her lap.

"Okay, I'll tell you what happened. Baseball *is* my thing, and when my mom and me came up from Jacksonville, we had hardly no money at all. So I couldn't buy equipment or nothin'. My mom has a job now, and she wants me to be a piano man or a preacher, but all I want to do is to play ball. So I had to get some money somehow. One day I met Ringo and some guys and they told me it was easy to get money if I wanted it, so I hung around with them for a while.

"Sure enough, they had plenty of money, and one day Ringo handed me that first baseman's glove and said, 'You can get this and lots more, if you want to work with us.' So I asked them what I had to do, and they said, 'Just be a watchman for us, and do some small jobs and soon the money will get better.' The watchman stuff was to watch their getaway bikes while they stole things, and the other job was mostly to lift things they needed from stores. They paid me some money for that and gave me things ... like your glove, Hawk."

"That's very sad," Panny said. "You let them turn you into a thief and an accomplice. But if you help us, you can get out of it. The police will appreciate anything you tell us."

"I don't want to go to jail. I just want to play baseball."

"Mr. Rizzuto will help you get on a good team," Hawk said. "You're a terrific player."

Elroy thought for a moment, and then said, "I don't know much about the Rippers. They told me that if I helped them I would get cut in on a big job they had planned. There's something happening on Monday night — tomorrow. I'm supposed to break into this warehouse with them. It ain't far from here. I can show you. They told me just where we'd look in this warehouse and what we we'd find.

"They said it was something called the O'Boyle container. Some judge — O'Boyle, I guess — passed away and left something valuable in there. Or maybe O'Boyle is the guy who's paying them to get the valuables for him. I dunno. But I have to help bring it out for them. It's a test for me, I guess, so I can be a gang member ... a real one."

Hawk looked at Panny, then at Martin. "If it's so valuable, I'm surprised they don't get it themselves. Why get Elroy to do it?" he asked.

Panny shrugged her shoulders. "Mr. Big maybe has a few rivals, so he passes the job to the Rippers and keeps his hands clean," she said. "Then the Rippers put the burden on Elroy. If he gets caught, he gets all the blame. A kid from down south is a good victim to set up. He has no friends and no support. They might even be planning to pin the whole thing on him, once they get what they want. I wonder what's in this O'Boyle container that's so valuable."

"Probably some jewellery or furs, or something like that," Albert said.

"But you're not doing this job alone, right, Elroy?"

"No, I'm meeting Ringo and a couple of guys. They're gonna show me the ropes, they said."

"Perfect!" Panny said. "Then we can set a trap. We have to be careful, though. These guys are dangerous. We'd better start planning now. Elroy, let's go over the location and the layout of the warehouse and get the time right so we can figure out how to deal with them. Albert, we'll get your cousin and the rest of the police in on this. We won't take too many chances, but we don't want to be sent home before the fun starts, do we? We want to catch these guys, and get Elroy in the clear. Well, it looks like we can take care of the school gang on Monday morning and finish off the street gang on the very same evening! Nice way to start the week — right, boys? This is turning into quite an adventure!"

Chapter 17

O'Boyle's Treasure

When he got home, Hawk was so excited he could hardly sit still. Luckily, his father put his behaviour down to the confrontation coming up with the Ferrets.

"You told your friends about that Charles's bullying, like I said?" Jim asked.

"Yeah, they were shocked. They didn't know anything about it."

"Well, don't you worry about a thing, son. I've got an appointment with Ms. Calloway before class even starts tomorrow. We're going to knock this Charles for a loop. Tonight, you have to finish the outline for your history talk. Ms. Calloway wants to see it before you deliver it, right? She's expecting it tomorrow, you told me."

"Don't worry, Dad, I'm nearly finished."

"Okay. And you just leave this Charles business to me."

Hawk got out the laptop he'd been using at his dad's and went over his talk. It seemed fine to him, even though he had to leave a lot out. He printed it and put it in his schoolbag to take in the morning.

Sleep didn't come easy that night, especially when his father came into his bedroom and told him he'd forgotten to pass on a message. Mr. Rizzuto had apparently telephoned earlier. He was going to pick up Hawk after school. "Something very important," he'd told Jim.

"You have a pretty busy life these days," his father said. Hawk thought guiltily that Jim didn't know the half of it.

He woke up bleary-eyed the next morning. His father, who had put on a jacket and a fresh white T-shirt, said he had to drop in at the Native Centre office for a few minutes. He'd be at the school, though, before Ms. Calloway got started.

"She's probably in for a shock," his father suggested.

"Not as big a shock as Charles, I hope."

When Hawk left for school a short time later he was both excited and a bit scared by his prospects — The Ferrets and Mr. Rizzuto, not to mention the Rippers hovering in the background. Hawk's heart beat fast as he walked, quickly leaving The Pocket and its bustling everyday life behind. When he saw his solid old red-brick school rising up among the trees at the end of the street, it seemed to him for the first time a real place of adventure. This might be the biggest day of his life, he realized. He hurried his pace and glanced up and down the street, looking for but not spotting his father's car.

When he arrived in the classroom everything seemed normal. Albert was busy doing something at his desk. Panny came over and asked if he'd finished his outline and he told her he had. Then Charles appeared, a confident smirk on his face. He slipped past Hawk's desk, whispering as he passed, "Morning, Princess. You'd better have that dollar ready by the first recess."

Ms. Calloway appeared at the door and the bell rang. The class settled down and Ms. Calloway asked if Hawk had the outline of his personal contribution ready.

He murmured a quite yes, and carried the paper up to her. She thanked him and placed it in her inbox. She hardly looked at him and Hawk wondered what was going on.

Minutes later, however, instead of the usual session of private "teacher talk," Ms. Calloway made an unexpected announcement.

"Pay attention, class! I have to go to the principal's office for a short while. Mr. Jackson is going to step in for me. Just do your work and pay attention to what he says. I'll be back as soon as I can."

Hawk waited with baited breath, and then she said it: "Oh, Charles, would you mind coming with me, please."

At first the boy didn't move, and just sat there looking puzzled. But after a few seconds he slowly got up and followed Ms. Calloway out of the classroom. Panny leaned over and whispered to Hawk, "Now the fat's in the fire!"

Mr. Jackson, a burly young teacher from down the hall, entered, smiling, and waved for the kids to be silent.

Ms. Calloway came back after the first recess, thanked Mr. Jackson for stepping in, and then called Hawk up to her desk. "I'd like to talk to you privately at recess," she told him. "I'd like you to tell me about all your conversations with Charles Wainright. Just tell me what he said to you and describe the contents of all of his messages. Don't mention this to anyone else in the class right now, please."

At the break, Hawk told her everything he could remember. She asked a few questions. After that, the day went on as usual. Charles didn't come back to class. Hawk didn't see his father. As he was leaving school, Panny approached him and said, "I wonder if Charles will be expelled."

"I hope so," Hawk said. "Otherwise I might get in big trouble."

"Not a chance of that," Panny said. "But look over there — isn't that your friend Mr. Rizzuto in the big car, waving at you as if his arm will fall right off?"

Hawk sprinted down the sidewalk and jumped into Mr. Rizzuto's car.

"Have I got news for you!" his friend said excitedly.

'What is it? What's happened?" All thoughts of Charles vanished from Hawk's mind.

"Let's go back to the shop and I'll tell you there."

They drove on in silence, although Hawk was bursting to ask questions. Only when they'd settled down in the back of the shop and Hawk was sipping a tall lemonade did Mr. Rizzuto go into action.

With a pleased smile and a few knowing nods of his head, he lifted a large manila envelope from a nearby shelf and spread out a bundle of papers, photographs, and computer scans on the big table in front of Hawk.

"It's about Babe Ruth's baseball," he said. "I think we've got a breakthrough. I think it's maybe a home run with the bases loaded in the last of the ninth."

Hawk said nothing, but nearly choked on his lemonade.

"Take it easy, kiddo." Mr. Rizzuto smiled. "This is no time for us to have to call 911. In fact, I'm going to give you 911 right there in your chair. You see, I heard from Mr. Wingate, and it's dynamite news."

"Did he find Babe Ruth's baseball?" Hawk stammered out.

"Not quite, but, listen, here's the story. Once upon a time — it was during the First World War, as I told you already — there was a baseball field out there at Hanlan's Point on Toronto Island. And yes, on a fine June morning in 1914 a young player named Babe Ruth did hit his first home run there. Oh, it must have been quite a scene — an amusement park, families having picnics, and the baseball game going on right beside them next to the lake. And, as Mr. Wingate has figured out, a good number of home runs hit back then went right into the lake. He also figured out that there were always kids swimming around out there, eager to grab anything that floated. But there was also someone else ..."

He paused and Hawk bent closer to catch every word.

"That's right!" Mr. Rizzuto continued. "There was an enterprising harbour rat, an Irishman with a little motor boat, a fellow named Danny O'Boyle who hung out around there. He was called 'Skimmer O'Boyle,' in fact, because he cruised around the lake picking up anything he thought was of value. He also paid kids, swimmers, divers, anyone, to find things for him. There was actually an article about this in the Toronto *Star* newspaper — it had a different name then — and Mr. Wingate found it.

"Anything O'Boyle could dredge up, he did, and I suspect he wasn't above helping some of the stuff get lost, if you see what I mean. Anyway, as the story goes, old Skimmer was on the lake almost every day. He had a great collection and was always hoarding things "for his old age," as he told the newspaper. But you know how it happens, and one day he drowned trying to salvage some cases of whiskey. That was not long after the Babe's home run in 1914.

"Skimmer's whole collection went to his wife, and later to his son and grandson. His son ignored his dad's treasures, but his grandson was pretty proud of old Skimmer — nice to have a colourful character in your family, so long as you don't have to live with them! And his grandson was quite the man — he became a judge and got very rich. Turned most of his estate over to the church, but his sister, who was a nun, got a houseful of mementos and family treasures, most of which she put in a warehouse somewhere in Toronto."

Hawk felt his pulse beat a little faster. *A warehouse somewhere in Toronto!*

"Mr. Wingate even managed to get a partial list of the O'Boyle effects," Mr. Rizzuto continued. The tally includes, it says, 'miscellaneous sporting goods, including items connected with football, hockey, soccer, and baseball.' Rumours have spread over the years — mostly since the judge's death — that there might be some valuable things in the O'Boyle collection. It seems that old Skimmer was relentless. He went out almost every day, and even mentioned picking up baseballs from the lake in the newspaper article they did on him at the time. No question that he was active in 1914, and salvaging any souvenirs he could get. And the islands were his favourite haunt, and sports gear one of his favourite trophies.

"Babe Ruth's baseball!" Hawk almost shouted. Then, in a calmer voice, he added, "But wouldn't the judge have known the value of the baseball?"

"The judge never got around to having the warehouse stuff properly evaluated. It was sorted out, but experts haven't seen it. He was thinking more of the family connection, and he probably assumed he had a stash of junk — old toys, sporting goods, beach umbrellas, bits of boating gear, with a couple of valuable items maybe shoved away in the boxes somewhere. And think about it. If one of those harbour kids picked up the baseball in the lake, or the Skimmer himself retrieved it, why should they make a fuss? The Babe only became famous later on."

"I'm thinking about that warehouse in Toronto," Hawk said. He thought of what he and his friends would be doing this very night, and shivered. *Could there be a connection? There had to be!* Elroy had mentioned the O'Boyle container. That's what the Rippers were after!

"I've been thinking about it, too," Mr. Rizzuto said. His face wore a serious expression. "You see, Mr. Wingate gave me this information early last Friday when I met him for brunch. And he also told me something a bit scary. Those other people he mentioned that were interested in the O'Boyle treasure — you remember, I told you about them before? He wouldn't tell me who they were when I first consulted him, but this time he told me something that worries me a bit."

Hawk sat up. "I think I know what it was," he said. "He told you that it was a Chinese group, headed by a very nice gentleman who drives an expensive antique car."

Mr. Rizzuto jumped from his chair. "Holy cow! How did you know that? What have you been up to, kid?"

"My friends and I have found out that there's a Chinese gang working with the Rippers, and that they may be about to use those street kids to break into a warehouse in Toronto, a warehouse down near the Studio District! They're after the O'Boyle container!"

Mr. Rizzuto gaped at him. "To steal the O'Boyle treasure? Maybe to get hold of Babe Ruth's lost baseball? But it's mine now! I just arranged to buy the whole package from Judge O'Boyle's widow! I couldn't take a chance that someone would beat me to it. I tracked her down and we made a tentative deal on Saturday morning. I'm about to become the rightful owner of that stuff and I want to know exactly *when* and *where* this robbery is going to take place! They haven't told me where the stuff is being kept, and I won't get all the final details until I meet with the widow and her lawyer later this evening."

Hawk stood up. "Tonight, Mr. Rizzuto. In a few hours we can find out everything. My friends know the area where the warehouse is. You have to be ready to come right over there — and bring your proof of ownership."

"Come right over where? Where do I have to show up?"

"Wherever I call you from, Mr. Rizzuto. And don't worry, the police will be there to help you out!"

Chapter 18

Walking into Trouble

A few minutes later Mr. Rizzuto led Hawk out to his car. “I don’t know about this,” he murmured. “I just don’t know. I still think we ought to call the police right away.”

Hawk smiled. “I thought you were supposed to stay clear of the police,” he reminded him. “Some of your family wouldn’t like it, remember?”

Mr. Rizzuto hung his head and looked a bit sheepish. “Well, yeah, that’s true. Maybe we don’t need the cops right away. But you tell me that your dad doesn’t know anything about this? Holy cow! Are you kids asking for trouble or what?”

The old man seemed very nervous. He frowned, shook his head, and pushed his straw boater to one side while he wiped his sweating brow with a paper towel.

"We're not asking for trouble, Mr. Rizzuto," Hawk assured him. "We're just planning things so the other guys have all the trouble."

"Yeah, yeah, I see what you mean, but you know the old saying — about how the best laid plans of mice and men can screw up something awful."

"Sure, but that's why Albert — he's one of the kids — is going to get his cousin in on this. His cousin is a policeman. But we've got to do it at the right moment — otherwise things may really get messed up, and our friend Elroy could be in danger."

"Well, let's hope you guys can recognize the right moment when you see it. I hope the right moment doesn't hit you in the face and give you a black eye. You get in touch with me as soon as you call the cops. I want to be there to check on my goods — maybe on *our* baseball!"

Not long after, Hawk stood on the sidewalk outside of his dad's house. He waved goodbye to the still-doubtful Mr. Rizzuto, then went inside, only to find that his dad hadn't come home yet. Hawk went up to his room and tried to read one of the books of Native legends that his dad had recommended, but he was far too excited to concentrate. Finally, just before dinnertime. Jim turned up. Hawk was relieved; his dad had a big smile on his face.

"Hey, Hawk, you should have seen that kid do some squirming. And his dad too! Ms. Calloway and Ms. Clarke are something else — a couple of powerhouses. And the principal went right along with them. That Mr. Wainright, Charles's father, he's some kind of big-shot lawyer and he tried to brush things off. He said his good little Charles was just bored in the class — not getting enough stimulation. Can you believe it? He tried to pass the buck to the teachers! But they shot that one down real quick. 'We have an open program and if Charles needs more stimulation he should be able to find it,' they told him. 'And if he can't find it in our classroom, then he might want to look for it elsewhere. It's really up to him — and you.'

"That's the kind of thing they told the guy, and he finally gave up. Charles is going to stay in your class, but he's going to have to apologize to everyone, including you, and be closely monitored. If he tries any more nasty stuff, he'll be out on his ear!"

Hawk felt a wave of relief as his father continued. "And you know something else, son. I think that kid was almost glad to be found out. I think the whole Ferret thing was bugging him, but he didn't know how to get out of it. It was a monkey on his back, but he deserved to suffer. He made other kids suffer. I just hope it's over now — for everybody."

"That's just great, Dad. I almost feel sorry for Charles. Maybe he'll be a good guy after all. Anyway, that's one gang taken care of!"

As soon as he said this, Hawk realized he'd made a mistake.

"You mean there's more than one gang you're dealing with?" his father asked.

"Yeah, of course." Hawk gulped and stammered out an explanation. "I mean, don't forget the

Rippers. In fact, I promised to meet some of the kids tonight — one of them knows a lot about what the Rippers are up to. And Albert, one of my friends, has a cousin who's a policeman. So we're going to talk Elroy into telling the police about the Rippers."

His father gave him a serious, searching look. "Who's Elroy?"

"One of the kids who might join the Rippers."

"So you kids are going to talk him out of it?? Hmmm, well, I guess that's all right. I hope you succeed. But what about dinner? You can't postpone it all night, you know. And don't forget that you have school tomorrow. I don't want to hear from your mother about how I've neglected you!"

"Oh, it's okay, Dad. I had a sandwich. And I might have another when I get back. And I won't be too late either." Hawk squirmed a bit. He knew his dad would be contacted if things dragged on, and luckily he'd hidden the glove Elroy had returned to him under his bed. His father wasn't likely to spot it there. Otherwise he'd have more explaining to do.

A few minutes later, Hawk was sprinting off in the direction of the nearest bus stop. Panny had decided they would meet down near the Studio District, not far from Lake Shore Boulevard. The warehouse that held the O'Boyle treasure was a short walk away. She'd gotten the warehouse address from Elroy and staked the place out on Google.

They would have to wait until dark for Elroy's break-in, but Panny would call or text all the parents a little later and invent some excuse, just to reassure them all that their kids were okay. Once that was done they would go into action, then call the police, who would arrive, they hoped, just in time to catch the Rippers.

The bus roared up and Hawk jumped on. Flopping down in his seat, eyeing the weary commuters and watching the busy streets slip by through the smeared windows, he began to wonder if he had really been guilty of deceiving his own father. After all, he had told him *most* of the truth, which hopefully was enough. And once the police caught the Rippers and got Elroy out of there, all would be forgiven — at least he hoped so.

Hawk jumped off the bus just before it turned into the heart of South Riverdale. He walked down toward Lake Shore Boulevard, keeping a sharp eye out as he trudged along a dreary stretch of vacant lots, low dingy buildings, and shabby warehouses. The sunlight, which had been strong and bright all day, seemed to sink and dissolve into this dusty confusion of blank streets and faceless facades. There were a few parked cars, but they looked forlorn, as if they had been abandoned forever.

At last he came to an intersection of four narrow streets. A small, boarded-up building on an opposite corner caught his attention. As Hawk came closer, he could just make out through the dirty, cracked windows a half-fallen and faded sign advertising shaves and haircuts. The boy's heart beat faster. This must be the place Panny had described — the place chosen for their "headquarters." But the empty streets, the lack of any sign of life, made him hesitate. For a moment he was frightened. He suddenly realized the danger. *What if the Rippers appeared and recognized him? What if a police car came by and asked him why he was wandering alone through this deserted neighbourhood?*

He shivered and had a strong impulse to turn and run. But just then someone called out his name, speaking in a kind of strangulated whisper that didn't prevent him from recognizing Martin Schiller's voice.

"Hey, Hawk! You idiot! Don't just stand there — get over here!"

A hand reached out through one of the barbershop's broken windows and waved a baseball cap at him.

Chapter 19

Trapped by the Rippers

Hawk scampered across the street, just as two cars appeared suddenly at the next intersection and headed in his direction. *Could one of the gangs be prowling in the area?*

The boy hurled himself forward, the baseball cap vanished and a big section of the patchy shop window swung back, making a convenient doorway. Hawk staggered in as the panel closed behind him. He blinked and looked around.

"I was sure you'd make it," Panny said. "I told the boys you would."

She was standing behind a couple of card tables that had been set up in the middle of a dreary room. Two portable lanterns sat on the tables, casting a spooky light on the maps, charts, notebooks, cellphones, walkie-talkies, and flashlights arranged there.

"Welcome to the Schiller Bunker," Martin said as he fastened the front panel and stepped forward to kick at a stray piece of glass.

"He gets to name it because he found it," Albert said. "Can you believe that he and his friends used to explore these buildings? You must have been desperate for play space," he added, shaking his head at Martin. He turned and winked broadly at the still-dumfounded Hawk.

The corners of the "bunker" were littered with junk — old metal, broken signs, rusted-out paint cans and tools, and a couple of frayed blankets lying among the broken glass, where it looked as if a homeless person might recently have slept.

"No, we didn't kick out some poor street person," Albert said, reading Hawk's thoughts.

"I hope there aren't any rats around," Hawk said.

"The rats are in the warehouse nearby," Panny said. "Or they soon will be. And when we hear from Elroy, we'll go rescue him."

Panny smiled, took a dog biscuit from a box, and held it out for Chew-Boy, who had crawled out of one of the dark corners to greet Hawk. "This is a dump all right," she said, with a glance at her watch. "Actually, the only reason I'm letting Chew-Boy run around is to keep the real rats away. I can't stand rats!"

She made a face and added, "But this a good place for us to work from. And now it's time to get down to business."

Hawk played with Chew-Boy for a minute while Panny continued her explanation. "It's seven-fifteen right now," she told them. "In a minute I'll send the first text messages to reassure our parents."

"Don't bother with my aunt," Martin said. "She doesn't text and she won't even notice that I'm still out."

Panny shrugged her shoulders. "Okay. Messages to my parents, to Albert's, and to Hawk's dad. Also a preliminary message to Albert's cousin, the police officer, just so he knows that we're up to something. But don't worry, I'll keep it low-key so he doesn't start searching for us. If he arrives too soon, our plan will be spoiled and Elroy could be in a mess."

"Suppose the Rippers have planned their robbery for the middle of the night," Hawk put in. "No matter what you tell them, all of our parents will go nuts waiting for us."

"It can't be the middle of the night," Panny said. "They're meeting Elroy very soon and they'll tackle the job just after they meet, I'll bet. They're not so dumb as to break in just when the watchmen and cops are most expecting break-ins."

She was already busy texting messages and in a very few moments had finished. "Now we have to wait for Elroy. It's all set up — all he has to do is press a button to dial my cell. He doesn't have to say a word. When I see the right number in front of me, I'll know he's in the warehouse and they're ready to start hauling away the O'Boyle loot."

"I just wish I knew what that loot was," Albert said. "Must be some kind of jewellery ... or gold maybe, or a Picasso painting. Judges can afford to buy that stuff."

Hawk, who'd been bursting with his news, spoke up. "It's none of those. I know exactly what they're after. Mr. Rizzuto and I have been chasing it all along. Now I just talked to him and he told me that he found out that Mr. Big has been chasing down the same thing. And it's not jewellery, or gold, or any kind of painting. It's something even better. It's the baseball Babe Ruth hit for his first home run!"

The kids gaped at Hawk, then glanced, astonished, at one another. The filthy, half-wrecked room was suddenly silent. Then Martin Schiller pursed his lips and let out an amazingly loud whistle, one that seemed to shake the dust and cobwebs in every corner.

"The baseball is that valuable?" the skeptical Albert wondered. "But how do they know it's the right one?"

"Scientific tests," Panny said. "The baseballs were made differently in those days and they can test the fibres and the stuffing and the stitching. Right, Hawk?"

"That's what Mr. Rizzuto thinks," Hawk said. "The ball was hit out of the old stadium at Hanlan's Point and probably landed in the lake. But there was a pack rat guy, the grandfather of Judge O'Boyle, who salvaged just about everything of any value from the lake, and it's a good bet that we might find that baseball with the rest of the judge's treasures. And you remember what Professor Sam said, Panny — the big gangs go after sports souvenirs. Even if there's a baseball and it's a forgery, they can probably get good money for it. And if it's the real thing, they might get a fortune."

"Wow, cry in your sangria, Picasso, this baseball may top some of your good prices," said Albert, who knew a lot about art and special drinks.

Panny passed out sandwiches and the kids waited impatiently for some signal from Elroy. They could see through the dirty glass of the windows that it was getting darker outside.

"Maybe the Rippers found your cellphone and are torturing poor Elroy right now," Albert said, giving the implacable Panny a doubtful look.

At that very moment Panny's phone rang with a jaunty tune. There was no one on the other end. "That's him!" she said. "Let's get going!"

She snapped a lead on Chew-Boy, handed out the flashlights, and proceeded to place a call to Constable Perkins, Albert's police connection. "Here, tell him what's happening, but don't give him the address just yet. He might mess everything up," she instructed, handing Albert the phone.

After being transferred and put on hold several times, Albert was finally connected to his cousin. A long conversation ensued and Panny grew impatient. "Hang up! We've got to get out of here!"

Albert shrugged his shoulders and ended the conversation. "I've got bad news," he said. "He assumed I was pulling a prank." Panny stamped her foot. "I didn't think of that," she muttered. "But it can't be helped — we've got to move in right now."

A few minutes later they were hurrying through a maze of narrow streets and blind alleys. Soon they could see a hulking row of old red-brick warehouses rising beyond an area of littered lots.

"We cut through here," she told them. They tramped along beside her — Hawk, Albert, and Martin — as she urged Chew-Boy forward on the lead. It was getting darker by the minute. When they reached the next street, they all stopped. Two cars were parked down the street to the left.

"There's someone in the first car — the SUV," Hawk said. "Maybe that's the getaway car, with a gang member watching. Won't he see us when we go in?"

"No, he won't," Panny said. "There's an alley that runs beside that big warehouse. The entrance is there. Just pretend we're playing some game and then duck into the alley when we get close enough — don't head straight for it."

She let Chew-Boy off the leash and they started throwing sticks for him to fetch. Toss by toss they came closer to the big warehouse. Soon they could see the alleyway. It was empty. Martin threw the last stick, Chew-Boy raced after it, and the kids followed on the dog's heels.

Halfway down the long alley, Panny called a halt. "There's the door Elroy mentioned," she said. "He was going to try to leave it open. Let's see!"

She swung the door outward; it creaked a little in opening. "All right," Panny whispered. "That's music to my ears. Albert, you stay here on watch. And call that stupid cousin of yours and get him over here! Come and warn us if that guy on the street decides to check us out."

"All right, boys, turn on your flashlights and let's go!" Panny and Chew-Boy led the way into the gloomy passage. The boys followed and Albert swung the door shut behind them. It was suddenly dark, but to Hawk's relief not quite pitch black, and the flashlights pierced the gloom ahead.

Hawk squeezed his light, wishing it was his father's Colt 45. But then he'd promised never to fire that weapon in anger. If his father could see him now, he thought, he'd set him straight very quickly. *Are you crazy — going into a place like that?* Hawk could hear Jim's condemning voice. He hoped Panny knew what she was doing.

With Chew-Boy now on his long leash, Panny led the way forward. They passed several closed doors and metal hatches that might have been lockers. Barrels had been stacked up along one side of the wall, and various dollies, carts, and slings hung on racks.

"Here's the first turn," Panny said quietly, gesturing with her flashlight. At a junction, small signs pointed the way in various directions — SECTION A, SECTION B, SECTION C.

Panny stopped and looked at her watch. "Elroy is supposed to head toward the main exit as soon as he can break free," she reminded them. "They'll come after him, and we can intercept them and tell them the place is surrounded and the cops are outside. Hopefully they'll just run for it — and meet Albert's cousin and the rest of the police outside."

"Assuming Albert gets his cousin over here," Martin said. "Assuming Albert's cousin believes the story. What happens if they don't come?"

As Martin spoke, a metal door in the wall beside him swung open. He was knocked off his feet and lay sprawled on the floor. A burly teenager, bare-armed and muscular and wearing a white cowboy hat, stood up in the flashlight beams. One of the Rippers!

He swore at them and growled, "What are you kids doing here?" Then, as Hawk ducked back against the wall, the teen took a step toward Panny.

Chew-Boy growled. Panny released him and he sprang forward. The teen groped at his belt, and, as the dog leapt up and bit his hand, a knife clattered to the floor.

"I'll kill that mutt!" he screamed. Hawk sprang over and kicked the knife away. The teen lurched after him, Chew-Boy snapping at his heels. Martin stuck out his foot and the teen crashed down. He swore again.

The corridor lights suddenly flashed on. Albert appeared, looking frightened. "That guy in the car's coming in. We're trapped in here!"

"Where's your stupid cousin?" Martin shouted.

A figure appeared in one of the side corridors. It was Elroy, scared and excited. "I got away, like you said!" he told Panny. "But Ringo's coming after me. Where's those police?"

Martin and Hawk had jumped on top of the angry teen, and Elroy started to help them, but the Ripper was very strong and they were having trouble holding him. Hawk spotted four or five barrel hoops; large metal rings that were hanging in a recess where the corridors met, and had an idea. He scrambled away, ducked into the recess, climbed up on an old barrel, and pulled down one of the hoops. But he froze as he heard the sound of footsteps coming down the side corridor. Seconds later, the dim lights revealed a familiar figure — Ringo! The boy stepped out of the shadows, spat harshly on the concrete, and pulled something from his belt — an ordinary crowbar. But in the Ripper's hand it looked menacing.

Ringo stood at the junction, in front of Hawk, who could almost touch his close-shaven, lumpish head, and the tattoos that marked his shoulders. Hawk could see the boy's neck muscles twitching as he shifted the crowbar from hand to hand.

At first sight of their adversary, Chew-Boy had started growling, and now the dog barked once, twice, at this new and frightening apparition. But Panny had picked up the feisty dog and held him in check as she whispered a few soothing words in his ear.

Ringo, however, had switched his attention at Elroy. Hawk could sense the piercing gaze directed at the boy, and he could see Ringo's arm muscles twitching as he squeezed the crowbar again and again, rocking forward on the soles of his feet as he did so.

"You turned on the lights, didn't you, smart boy?" Ringo asked, still glaring at Elroy. "You set this up to catch us. You sold us down the river for these twerps."

The burly teen the boys had wrestled to the floor picked up his knife, climbed to his feet, and chimed in. “What are we gonna do with them, Ringo?” he growled. “Should we lock ’em up in one of the cases? They can rot there for a few years and see how they like it.”

“I was thinking of that,” Ringo said. “Stash ’em away forever in a black box. But not this one, not this boy …” He waved his crowbar at Elroy and continued. “This one we’ll take along to Mr. Big. Mr. Big will have a good idea of how to get rid of this trash.”

Hawk shuddered and pressed himself flat against the wall, wishing he could make himself invisible.

Ringo laughed and moved forward. Martin and Albert stepped up beside Elroy. Panny joined them, holding Chew-Boy — all the kids but Hawk crowding in together.

“Hey, Sterling,” Ringo called out, suddenly addressing his sidekick. “You see those bags on the pegs over there? … Yeah, on the wall there! Grab one for me, will ya.”

The burly Ripper moved obediently and fetched one of the bags. Ringo waved him closer, took the bag from him and inspected it, running his fingers with satisfaction along the strings that closed it tight at the top. Then he bent over and whispered something in his sidekick’s ear as he handed the bag back to him. Leaning over from his perch, Hawk tried to catch the words, but he was much too far away to hear anything.

Slowly, Sterling backed toward the little group of friends that stood nervously watching. When he got very close, and they began to pull away, he whirled round, facing them, and before Panny could twist away he'd seized her and started to wrench the snarling Chew-Boy out of her grasp.

Martin and Elroy edged forward to help, but Ringo approached them with a threatening gesture. "Just touch him and you get this crowbar through your skull!" he snarled.

Meanwhile, Sterling had got hold of the squirming, yelping Chew-Boy and stuffed him head-first into the bag. He pulled the drawstrings tight, and when Panny attacked him, he knocked her down.

The others gasped and stirred, but Ringo swung the crowbar, threatening them.

It was now or never, Hawk decided. He could see a tall, thin figure, the third Ripper who had been watching from the car, coming slowly up from the entrance. They were trapped now, and there was only one hope. He tightened his grip on the barrel hoop, jumped down from his perch, and flung it with all the force he could muster at Ringo's back.

It hit the mark. Ringo screamed, swore, and staggered forward. Howling in pain, he dropped the crowbar, grabbed hold of the bag, and yanked it from Sterling's grasp.

"Pick up the crowbar! Let's flatten these stupid kids!"

Suddenly, from nearby came muffled shouts and the blare of voices as two small figures in blue appeared far down the passage near the entrance.

"STOP! DROP THOSE WEAPONS! YOU KIDS! OUT OF THE WAY. MOVE IT, NOW!"

It was two uniformed Toronto policemen. They approached the group, waving and shouting.

"YOU THREE BIG BOYS, DROP YOUR WEAPONS AND LINE UP AGAINST THE WALL. YOU'RE UNDER ARREST!"

Ringo swore and ran toward the open panel in the wall, swinging the bag, stuffed with the yelping dog, in front of him.

Sterling made as if to follow, but Martin tackled him, and Elroy helped pin him down.

"Ringo's escaping!" Panny shouted, and, picking herself up, she ran after him. Hawk tried to cut him off, but Ringo was too fast for them.

The Ripper sprang through the doorway and into the darkness beyond.

They followed, plunging into the darkness of a narrow corridor. Then they heard a clank, as if an iron door had slammed shut just in front of them. They groped forward. Hawk's fingers touched a metal door but the cold handle wouldn't budge.

"He's locked it — he'll get away!" Hawk groaned.

"He's got Chew-Boy! We've got to catch him." Panny grabbed Hawk's arm and led him back to the main corridor.

Hawk breathed a big sigh of relief. The policemen had come running up and shoved the other two Rippers against the wall.

As they systematically searched them, Panny lost her cool and started shouting. "What are you doing? The big fish has got away! And he's got my dog. He might hurt him. WHY ARE YOU JUST STANDING THERE?"

Albert smiled weakly, nodded at Panny and the boys, and with a glance at one of the policemen, announced quietly, "This is my cousin, Stanley Perkins."

Chapter 20

Pursuit in the Dark

"Thanks for coming," Panny said, making an effort to calm herself, "but you're a little late. The head Ripper is escaping right now. He's locked the passage doorway and we can't follow him. And he has my dog!"

Elroy ran over. "Panny, I know where he's got to. They showed me the escape routes, remember? Just follow me and we'll get him!"

Officer Perkins, a very round man with goggle eyes, huge hands, and a rather large red nose, objected. "Now, just a minute, kids! You've already pushed things too far. You — hey, wait a minute! You can't leave right now."

Nobody paid any attention, however, and the four kids, with Elroy in the lead, tore off and away down one of the branching passageways. Only Albert stayed where he was.

"Look at it this way, Cousin Stanley," he said, "I'll be their representative. I'll stay here and explain everything. You can take notes on the case, and if they need help, I'm sure one of them will get in touch. It's not just any dog. It's Chew-Boy they're after. Anyway, I tipped you off on this one, and you'll get a promotion for sure when you bring these guys in."

Officer Perkins glared at his cousin. "Promotion? I'll be lucky not to get suspended. What do you think, Horse?" The other officer, who was even bigger than Albert's cousin, grunted. "If they come back with that Ringo character, we might get away with a reprimand, but if he happens to murder them … it won't go well for us."

Albert gasped and stared at him. "Gosh, do you think it's even possible?"

Elroy, Panny, Hawk, and Martin charged at full speed down a dimly lit corridor that ran to the west side of the huge warehouse.

"We'll catch him!" Elroy reassured them, breathing hard as he ran. "All the corridors have stairwells and elevators leading down to the basement. The only exit is on the west side. There's a long basement that runs right across the building. After he locked the door on you, he went down a stairwell, then he must've cut back west. We should be right behind him when we get down there."

"Is there anywhere he could have dumped Chew-Boy?" Panny asked. "An open sewer, a furnace — something horrible like that?"

"No — nowhere," Elroy assured her. "He's using him for a hostage, I guess."

"If he opens that bag, Chew-Boy will bite his hand off," Panny said angrily.

"Once he gets outside, I bet he'll head for the car we saw," Hawk told them. "Or, if the police have arrived there by then, he'll probably just walk off somewhere to get a taxi."

"Luckily, it's deserted out there," Panny said. "Otherwise we'd never find him."

They sprinted along until they came to a dull red light shining on the right side of the corridor.

"That's the stairs," Elroy shouted. "I just hope they ain't locked!"

They pushed easily through the heavy doors and bounded down the dusty, semi-dark stairwell. At the bottom they turned and entered another long hallway, this one at basement level.

"There's the entrance. You can see some lights out there. It leads to a ramp, and that will take us up to the street. That was supposed to be our getaway route."

"Whatever happened to the watchman?" Martin asked.

"He's locked up at the front in an old closet. I gotta remember to tell the police that."

"We can't be far behind him now," Martin gasped.

"Half a block at most," Elroy said.

"Do you hear some noise out there?" Panny asked. "I thought the streets would be deserted."

"I can't understand it," Elroy said. "There ain't nobody in these parts at night. But I see lights movin' and flashin' too. Could be a fire or something. That's the last thing we need!"

They finally reached the door and pushed out onto a low, sloping ramp. The street was slightly above them. They could hear voices, a multitude of them, and they saw windows lit, the lower stories of the old buildings being swept by lights.

"Sure ain't a prayer meeting," Elroy said.

At the top of the ramp they could see the street. A large bus, its lights flashing, had climbed the sidewalk and plowed into a lamppost, which was bent but still standing. Thin wisps of smoke drifted up from the vehicle's engine. A crowd milled around, mostly women, middle-aged and clearly distraught. They were talking away while a couple of men worked over a figure lying prone on the street. A police car was parked nearby. It had all the appearances of an accident that had just happened. The sound of an approaching ambulance could be heard in the distance.

Elroy stopped, took in the scene, and looked at the others. "Bad luck. With all this distraction, he'll get free for sure."

"If he's able to get free, that is," Martin said. "That bus hit someone. Who do you think it might be?"

Panny sprang to life. "Ringo! Then what about Chew-Boy?" She took off in the direction of the bus with the boys following close behind.

When they reached the fringes of the crowd, they stopped. Some women drifted over, eyeing them curiously.

"Where did you kids come from? Are you his friends?"

"Who's friends?"

A tall, cool-looking woman in jeans told them that a boy had been struck by the bus. A teenager. "He's not dead, don't worry," she said. "But we're all a bit ticked off because we're going to be late for the dog show. And we came all the way from Buffalo, New York, to be part of it.... Not that I don't feel sorry for the boy...."

The kids stood amazed as a second woman added, "Not that I blame the driver. Although he admitted that he got lost. We should be on a highway, not in the middle of these back streets. You do have speedways in Toronto, I assume?"

"Sure do!" Elroy said. "And we're off on one right now!"

The three kids sprinted forward. "He's got to have survived!" Panny prayed. "My poor Chew-Boy!"

When they got to the scene of the accident, the kids reassured themselves with a glance that it was, in fact, Ringo lying on the road. He wasn't dead, that was clear, as he was yelling at one of the officers to leave him alone. But there was no sign of a little white dog.

Then, just as one of the other officers was shooing them away, the kids noticed something wonderful.

There, unmistakably, was Chew-Boy, sitting on the lap of a grey-haired man in a raincoat, receiving loving attention from five or six ladies, who were petting and talking to the baffled but pleased animal with an affection that even the most pampered lapdog would have envied. A torn, frazzled white bag lay in the gutter beside the group.

"Chew-Boy!" Panny called out as she ran over to her friend. He recognized her at once and jumped into her arms, as joyfully as he always had.

When they got back to the warehouse, the corridors were crowded with uniforms, and as the police probed everywhere the whole place came alive with light and sound. Word had spread quickly about the fate of Ringo, who had been seriously, but not fatally, injured. The other two Rippers, scowling and swearing, were handcuffed and led away. Once they were gone, the police had all the kids sit down, and a police psychologist started asking for their names and home addresses and phone numbers.

"But what about Skimmer O'Boyle's treasure?" Hawk asked. "It belongs to Mr. Rizzuto. Babe Ruth's baseball may be in there!"

The psychologist, a gentle-looking woman in a plain blue suit, gave him a blank look. "I think you've had enough excitement for one night," she told him. "Your parents are being called and I'm sure they're all anxious to see you safely at home. Just take a deep breath and relax and we'll take care of everything."

Her reassuring words made Hawk twice as frantic. But at this point Constable Perkins intervened. "It's all right, Dr. Jones. I know what the boy's taking about.... My cousin Albert explained it to me. Albert called Mr. Rizzuto and he and his lawyer are on their way here now. Meanwhile, I think we'll all be here for a while until we get everything sorted out. The best news is that you kids will likely all get the morning off school tomorrow."

Panny, who was sitting nearby, cut in. "That's not such good news," she said. "We love school."

The constable sighed and shrugged his shoulders.

Chapter 21

What's in That Box?

A couple of hours later, Hawk arrived in a police car at his dad's place on Condor Avenue. Jim was waiting for him on the sidewalk in front of the house. He frowned and shook his head, but gave Hawk a hug before leading him inside.

"You are one stupid boy," he said. "Brave maybe, and intelligent, but also a damned fool!"

Hawk could see that although his father was a bit angry at him, and obviously had been worried, he was — in some funny way — very impressed.

When they sat down in the living room and Hawk had a glass of juice in hand, his father said quietly, "You weren't honest with me, Hawk. That's bad. It went fine when you told me about Charles and the Ferrets. I helped you with that one. You should have done the same in this case — even more so! If we're gonna be pals, from now on you have to be honest, and you have to trust me."

Hawk sniffed, swallowed a mouthful of juice, and fought back tears. "Yeah, Dad, I understand."

Jim cleared his throat, smiled briefly, and said, "Besides me worrying, there's your mother. She called tonight and I had to pretend everything was fine. She wants you to call her tomorrow, and what you tell her is up to you. But I suggest you save the detailed story until you see her in person."

"Sure, Dad."

"Okay, then. Get some rest. Just lie low for a couple of days. No friends, just some reading and quiet reflection. But you'll work on your schoolwork while you're here. Call it a punishment, a grounding if you like. It's for your own good.

"Your friend Mr. Rizzuto called me to apologize, and he explained that he wanted to set up a meeting and was wondering if he could hold it here — apparently it concerns you and your friends and the goings-on tonight. It'll be first thing in the morning, before school, in a couple of days. You can get on with life after that. But for now, just go upstairs and get some sleep."

Of course, Hawk found that "getting some sleep" was not so easy. He kept seeing the warehouse and its seemingly endless corridors, the blank walls, and shadowy recesses. He heard the clank of metal, the curses of the Rippers, the shouts of the police. He saw Ringo's tattooed arm swinging the crowbar.... *Could he duck in time?*

No! He screamed and woke suddenly, sweating and trembling. When he finally lay back down, he drifted off into a deep, peaceful sleep.

The next two days passed in a kind of dream. Jim allowed Hawk a few phone calls and he was glad to hear that his friends were all doing fine — Panny and Chew-Boy, Martin, Elroy, and Albert (though Albert was in quite a bit of trouble with his parents). On the third day Hawk was up early, and ate a hasty breakfast with his father before the guests began to arrive.

Panny zoomed up on her bicycle (green panniers today). "Where's the loot?" she joked, adding, "Hey, I miss school already!" Martin turned up with Elroy and they played catch in the backyard and talked about baseball, just as if they were old friends.

Then a small white moving truck arrived and parked on the narrow street in front of Jim's house. Two men got out. One of them was Chick Ciccarelli, wearing the old number 10 on his T-shirt. He and his helper searched through the large packing case in the back of the van and hauled out two smaller square containers, each about the size of an old-fashioned steamer trunk. These they brought into the house, just as Mr. Rizzuto drove up in his red van.

He jumped out of the vehicle, shook hands with Jim, and gave Hawk a hug.

"I saved it, kid. I saved it for you to see. We'll open it inside, when the gang's all here."

At that moment another car drove up, a small Mercedes, and two men got out. Mr. Rizzuto introduced his lawyer, Mr. Sverov, a stocky man dressed in a blue suit and tie, and Hal Hodges, a TV reporter in jeans and T-shirt. Hodges immediately hauled an enormous video camera out of the car.

"Everything documented, everything legal — that's my motto," said Mr. Rizzuto.

Another bicycle appeared — it was Ms. Calloway, who greeted Hawk with a big smile. "Well, you've been busy," she said. "I'm glad it all worked out."

"I don't think I'll do that again," Hawk told her sheepishly.

"No, that wouldn't be such a good idea. You can talk to the class about it this afternoon — you and Panny and Albert — and tell them what you learned from your experience. What's responsible and what's not. Ms. Clarke will be there, too. She wants to hear all about it, but this morning she's busy in Room 21."

Panny came out and greeted Ms. Calloway. "I don't think Albert's mother wants to let him come today," she said. "She's still a bit upset about the other night. Maybe if you called her, Ms. Calloway?"

Ms. Calloway smiled. "I guess I can give it a try."

Hawk and Panny followed her inside. The two boxes had been set up on the living floor. The cameraman was already filming, and the lawyer was flipping through some legal-looking papers.

"We can start with the second box while we're waiting for Albert," Mr. Rizzuto said. "I don't think it's the one, but we have to be sure. The records just say 'miscellaneous, including sports memorabilia.' Why don't you open it up for us, Chick."

Ciccarelli, equipped with a hammer, pliers, crowbar, and other tools, started work. Hawk winced a bit at the sight of the crowbar.

The lock was soon sprung open and Chick lifted the lid. All eyes were on the small, wrapped packages he brought out.

Mr. Rizzuto unwrapped each parcel himself. "One Spalding tennis ball, slightly warped," he began. "No apparent value."

He went on unwrapping the little bundles one by one: "One polo mallet, good condition. One very old pair of binoculars, water-damaged. One bag of golf balls — no apparent value. One pair of old-fashioned roller skates. One beach blanket, one folding umbrella. One bag of advertisements, programs, and so on for Hanlan's Point Amusement Park — pretty faded but these might be interesting.... And that seems to be it. Boy, I sure hope the other box has something more exciting than this pile of junk!"

At this point they stopped to have juice, coffee, and doughnuts. Albert arrived, and rather shamefacedly explained that his mother had made him swear not to go on any more unannounced "adventures."

Then they proceeded to open the second box. Hawk watched nervously as Chick removed the lock. *Was this the end of his great dream of finding the Babe Ruth baseball?*

Hal Hodges, the cameraman, was still filming.

Mr. Rizzuto peered into the box and held up crossed fingers. He unwrapped the first parcel and drew out what appeared to be a crumbling towel or rag. An ancient yellowed paper fluttered down. Panny picked it up and Mr. Rizzuto signalled her to read it. "Rowing trunks belonging to the internationally famous rower and later proprietor of Hanlan's Point Hotel, Ned Hanlan," she announced.

Panny giggled and looked around. "Don't know how the bidding will go on that one, Mr. Rizzuto."

"Well they might be worth something," pronounced Mr. Sverov. "If they don't fall apart first."

"This looks more promising," said Mr. Rizzuto. With a weak smile, he lifted his hat and dabbed at his sweating forehead. He had picked up a square box, not large, but big enough to hold a baseball. Hawk held his breath as Mr. Rizzuto tore away the paper. From the box he pulled a round object, swathed in a kind of linen.

"They didn't have cellophane in those days," Albert informed them, "or plastic wrapping."

"It looks like a baseball!" Mr. Rizzuto shouted. Then, tossing the object up and down in his hand, he added, "It feels like a baseball." He tore at the swathing, and as the wrapping fell away, Hawk and Elroy chanted in unison, "And it *is* a baseball!"

There it was at last — a baseball in Mr. Rizzuto's trembling hands. *But was it THE baseball*?

"It's a very old ball," he said. "It's a professional ball. It's been swatted hard at least once. Flat seams, not like today's baseballs. Now let me see what that paper says."

Inside the box was a note. Hawk, peering over Mr. Rizzuto's shoulder, saw that it was handwritten in a script that was both crude and ancient-looking — he guessed that the note dated quite far back. Certainly he'd never seen anything like it, except in photographs of old documents, like treaties, wills, and deeds.

As the boy was pondering this, Mr. Rizzuto seemed to go manic. He screamed, jumped up and down, waved his arms, and would have dropped the precious baseball if Mr. Sverov had not made a splendid dive across the floor to catch it.

"I hope this really is the one you're looking for," the lawyer murmured, handing his client the old ball. "I just tore my best suit to rescue it."

"It's the one! It's the one!" Mr. Rizzuto shouted. "Just listen to this, everybody."

They all drew closer as Mr. Rizzuto read from the paper: "This baseball recovered from water near Hanlan's Point by young swimmer, 13 June, 1914. Paid youth 10 cents. Hit by Providence Grays player, name unknown. Try to resell to Leafs. Otherwise retain and store."

"That's the Toronto Maple Leafs *baseball* team," Mr. Rizzuto explained. Thank God those cheapskates didn't buy it back!" He turned to Hawk and stuck out his hand. Hawk shook his hand, danced away, then slapped hands in celebration with his father and all his friends. "Are we going to be rich?" he asked Mr. Rizzuto.

"You just might be," said Mr. Sverov.

"You can bet your bottom dollar we'll be rich!" cried Mr. Rizzuto "The date fits, the team fits, the ball fits like a charm. We've done it. We had the faith and we've done it. We've found Babe Ruth's lost baseball!"

Chapter 22

Friends and Relations

The next day a television report on the great discovery was broadcast all over Canada. RIVERDALE KIDS FIND FAMED RUTH BASEBALL trumpeted one of the newspapers. Skeptics immediately appeared, questioning the authenticity of the ball. “A ball fished out of the lake and missing for decades? — sounds fishy to me,” wrote one testy columnist.

Mr. Rizzuto, however, was no fool. Weeks later the baseball was still being analyzed by experts, lab tests would soon be released, and everything pointed to the likelihood of this being the ball hit by the Great Bambino. “If it’s not the real deal, we’ll still make a fortune,” he assured Hawk. “I’ve already been offered a cool million, no questions asked, by a Japanese collector. I rejected it, of course. I’m holding out for a *couple* of million.”

Hawk read the papers and was thrilled by the pictures and by the prospect of making a fortune, but he was sorry that the baseball had disappeared again. He wanted to look at it, hold it in his hands, and tell himself over and over that he'd helped find this very special treasure. It seemed as if they had found it, only to have it spirited away again into another kind of never-never land. His father tried to reassure him. Together, they looked at the many pictures Hal Hodges had taken of the baseball, and at one in particular in which Hawk was holding the ball up in front of him, a triumphant smile on his face.

"That's the idea!" Jim told him. "Be happy because you had a chance to get in touch with something unique, to hold it in your hands. Just look at that baseball," he said to Hawk, pointing at a blow-up of the same photograph. "It's a piece of horsehide and cork and stitching shaped in a little circle. And what's so special about that little circle? I'll tell you what! It connects you to the past, to another world, to a famous player who played a great part in baseball history. When you see that ball, you're looking at a time that's gone forever, a time that was good in some ways, but very bad in others.

"Just think. Your friend Elroy could never have played baseball with the pros in those days — blacks weren't allowed. You and I would have been sent off to some horrible residence school to be 're-educated' and abused by white men. Panny and her relatives wouldn't even have been allowed into the country, or if they made it here, would have been stuck with some menial job. An Irishman like Skimmer O'Boyle would have been sneered at and never allowed into the houses of some well-off Toronto folk.

"Today, when you and I look at a little circle like that baseball, we ought to think of the Earth, the globe itself. This old Earth has shrunk some since those old days — it seems almost as easy to get a view of the whole big globe as of that small baseball. And you know something, Hawk? The whole human race — people all over the planet — are claiming a good life for themselves these days. Everybody wants to be respected, and, sure enough, everyone who tries to live right *deserves* to be respected — and helped. If you get some money for this little round globe of a baseball, this souvenir, you should think about that big globe and how every age has its challenges. Don't just think about getting money. Think about how, when you grow up, you can help make the world a much better place to live in, so we don't go back to the *bad* times of Babe Ruth's 'good old days.'"

Storm Cloud, who had rushed back from Ottawa after Hawk's adventure, very upset over his dangerous expedition, had soon gone back to the capital. Now that the baseball was deemed valuable, she appeared in Riverdale again to congratulate Hawk. "I always knew my son would be famous," she told him. "But I didn't know it would happen when you were only ten years old. You have to be careful, though, when you sell that baseball. When they find out you're a Native, they'll be sure to try to cheat you."

"Don't worry, Mum, everybody's been great. And Mr. Rizzuto is very smart. You know the baseball is going to be on display at the new Yankee Stadium. All of us kids are getting a free trip to the stadium, too. And Mr. Rizzuto is going down to visit his daughter. They're going to be friends again after all these years."

"That's only sensible, Hawk. Parents should always be friends with their children. Otherwise, what's the world coming to?"

"I'm just glad that you don't have to sell trinkets in the street anymore, Mum. I'm glad that I can stay in Toronto and visit you sometimes in Ottawa. I love my school and my class. I finally gave my talk on the Ojibway-Cree. I showed them drawings that I did myself, I played CDs of authentic music, and I told some great stories that I got from Dad. I did tons of research. I got an *A* in presentation, creativity, imagination, and originality, *and* the class questions didn't scare me like I thought they would. That's an *A*, Mum, not a *P* like Mrs. MacWhinney gave me."

"That's great!" Storm Cloud gave her son a hug. "You take after your mother.... And I never sold 'trinkets,' by the way. They were tiny art pieces. Of course, I haven't got time to do that anymore. I'm too busy organizing events and protests. They really need me up in Ottawa. I've got a great apartment, too, and I can't wait for you to come and visit. Maybe we can go on a march together."

A few days later the kids were in Professor Sam's apartment, telling him about their adventures. Panny's cousin listened eagerly and even took notes — after all, he was a crime expert, and was already collecting information on their case.

"This is great stuff," he assured them. "I'm almost glad you didn't take my advice and stay away from that Ripper gang. It was dangerous, but you did have a real adventure. Does anybody know what's happened to the gang members?"

"My cousin Stanley — he's a policeman, the one who rescued us — he told me a few things," Albert said. "It seems that the Ripper boys, including Ringo, are going to give information on Mr. Big and his operations in exchange for reduced sentences. I'm not supposed to talk about that, though."

"That's okay," Sam reassured him. "We all know how to keep a secret, don't we?"

"Hawk does, for sure," Panny said. "He had to live with some pretty dangerous secrets, like the Ferrets trying to put the squeeze on him, and our adventure at the warehouse, and at least one special secret, too, like the search for the Babe Ruth ball. How did you do it, Hawk-boy?"

Hawk thought for a moment, and then told the kids, "Well, it wasn't easy, but then I had to learn to trust my friends, my teachers, and my dad. I paid attention to what my dad said about having an inner power. It's great when your friends and family and your teachers back you up. That's when the world stops being a scary place."

He looked around the room and grinned. "But let's eat the rest of this food. Martin and Elroy and I have to play baseball today. We're starting in the Little League pretty soon and we want to be as strong as possible. Right, guys?"

Martin agreed and Elroy nodded. Chew-Boy barked and stood on his hind legs.

The kids laughed. "Did you teach him to do that?" Elroy asked Panny.

She smiled. "Of course not! Let's get one thing straight. Chew-Boy has a mind of his own. Of course, now and then he obliges me — like when I ask him to catch people by the ankles."

"Let's hope that doesn't happen again for a while," Hawk said.

Chew-Boy barked again, as if to say "me too!" The kids laughed, and went back to eating their dumplings and egg rolls.

Acknowledgements

I would like to thank Michael Carroll, editorial director and associate publisher at Dundurn, and, like me, a great baseball fan, for his encouragement and support of this project. Also, Dr. Burf Kay, a Riverdale resident, for his expertise on his home neighbourhood and his suggestions for changes. Any lingering mistakes about the Riverdale scene are not his fault. Like many fiction writers who set their stories in real places, I have taken pains to be accurate, but I have also felt free to do some inventing and juggling to suit my story. All the characters in *The Boy from Left Field* are imagined and none are based on a real person — any resemblance to actual people is purely coincidental.

The description of the "gifted" classroom that is Hawk's salvation is, however, based on my own experience at Ottawa's Mutchmor School, even though none of the students are portrayed in my book. The two team-teachers of the grade four class I often visited were marvellous exponents of the "multiple intelligences" approach. They encouraged imagination and creativity, and taught their students to develop their talents without apology, but to respect those who had different skills. Competition was acceptable, but the achievements of all were to be celebrated. Intellectual precision and enthusiasm were encouraged, yet the body — and physical exercise — were not neglected. Issues of classroom behaviour and morality were important. It was also considered essential for the students to understand the world outside, the whole globe, to learn about the environment, for example, or to know how to read the media, and also to value diversity. Both teachers in this classroom had previously worked with special education students from more disadvantaged groups, and they found parallels between the needs of the most gifted and the more challenged. For a while, at least, their unique program escaped the red tape and meddling of the school bureaucracy, much to the delight of the fulfilled and grateful children and their impressively committed and often demanding parents. Adults who knew what went on in Room 27 saw it as an inspiring place and would have loved to experience it themselves when they were children —this writer counts himself among them.

Finally, I would like to thank my Dundurn editor, Allison Hirst, who read this text with care and helped shape it into its present form. As with all of my books for young people, I have tried to please my audience, and love it when they respond to my stories, but, as usual, this one is really for the wide-eyed child in me.

Also by Tom Henighan

Doom Lake Holiday
9781550028478
$12.99

A summer holiday in a remote corner of Ontario's Rideau Lakes turns into a nightmare when Chip and Lee are drawn into a complex web of past and present; they struggle to make sense of these ancient mysteries, aided by a visiting anthropologist and a beautiful young woman who lives on an island with her reclusive and powerful grandfather.

Demon in My View
9781550026566
$12.99

With North America left in ruins by years of war, terrorism, ecological destruction, and marauding motorcycle gangs terrorizing the homeland, young Toby Johnson must travel with his dog across the dangerous countryside. A retelling of the biblical Book of Tobit, *Demon in My View* is a powerful breakthrough novel.

Viking Terror
9781550026054
$12.99

When Rigg and Ari hunt a marauding wolf in medieval Greenland, they get more than they bargained for. Their skill and courage are pitted against wily adversaries, with the survival of their people at stake.